Simon Murtagh, born in Kent, England, is a first-time author. He is passionate about political, social and economic issues. When he is not painting or writing, he enjoys a good tale, movies, food, drink and good company. He now lives with his wife, Karen, in beautiful British Columbia, Canada.

For Beth.

Simon Murtagh

LITTLE DEATH

AUSTIN MACAULEY PUBLISHERS
LONDON · CAMBRIDGE · NEW YORK · SHARJAH

Copyright © Simon Murtagh (2020)

The right of Simon Murtagh to be identified as author of this work has been asserted by him in accordance with section 77 and 78 of the Copyright, Designs and Patents Act 1988.

All rights reserved. No part of this publication may be reproduced, stored in a retrieval system, or transmitted in any form or by any means, electronic, mechanical, photocopying, recording, or otherwise, without the prior permission of the publishers.

Any person who commits any unauthorised act in relation to this publication may be liable to criminal prosecution and civil claims for damages.

This is a work of fiction. Names, characters, businesses, places, events, locales, and incidents are either the products of the author's imagination or used in a fictitious manner. Any resemblance to actual persons, living or dead, or actual events is purely coincidental. Austin Macaulay Publishers will not be liable for any and all claims or causes of action, known or unknown, arising out of the contents of this book.

A CIP catalogue record for this title is available from the British Library.

ISBN 9781528925792 (Paperback)
ISBN 9781528964449 (ePub e-book)

www.austinmacauley.com

First Published (2020)
Austin Macaulay Publishers Ltd
25 Canada Square
Canary Wharf
London
E14 5LQ

Cover illustration by Graham Chorny.

Contents

The Beginning	12
The Islands	16
The Emissary	19
The Rhyme and the Reason	23
The Old Woman	25
The Hill Tribes	27
The Lizard	32
The Gift	61
The Boy	77
The Message	79
The Old Man	110
The Question	112
The Dream	121
The Letter	127
The Return	132

The Heralds	**153**
The Desolator	**162**
Epilogue	**178**

Whilst much of what you hear will seem familiar, you should know this: this is not your Earth. It is an earth; it is Earth, just not the one of your intimacy or understanding.

The Beginning

The last rays of the setting sun were streaming through the windows of the cedar-lined room making the walls glow. The red and orange tones in the lumber made the room seem warmer than it actually was. The man dressed in white sitting behind the large oaken desk could see his hands turning blue. He formed them into gnarled sinuous fists and breathed on them, but it made no difference, they were still frigid.

He pushed himself away from his desk, the small brass wheels of the plush leather chair squealed as he did. He shuffled over to the large, red brick fireplace and threw a log onto the grate while cursing his poor circulation. The sombre black slate clock with the delicate porcelain face struck a single chime to mark the arrival of eight-thirty.

The dry log had ignited almost immediately, crackling and spitting as it did, sending a shower of sparks recklessly up the chimney. He turned away from the heat and placing his hands in the small of his back, stretched until his bones popped. As he settled back behind his desk, he was joined in the room by a valet who skirted the walls, lighting candles as he went. He exited the room as silently as he had entered it.

The man had no time to re-acquaint himself with his solitude as the door opened again almost immediately, and a red-faced man who had clearly been running came panting into the room. "My lord," he gasped, placing his sweaty palm on the desk trying to catch his breath. "Beneath the old oak on Gallows Hill…"

The other man raised his hand, "You're making no sense, slow down, order your thoughts; now begin again."

"Apologies, my lord," the red-faced man stuttered, "I have just received a report from the sisters at Gallows Hill, they said they have found…" he paused as if reluctant to finish his sentence, "they said they have found a Summer Child." The man in white listened intently, making no comment nor interruption. "After the storm last evening, the old oak inside the convent walls fell, and there she was in among the roots and earth."

The other man was standing once more. "She…" he repeated softly, "she was alone?"

The red-faced man nodded by way of confirmation. "More than that, my lord, she is a baby!"

A carriage with four horses was hastily readied and soon on its way to Gallows Hill, no more than an hour away without stopping. The moonless night was now deep and dark, and the lanterns on the carriage barely lit the road at all. The convent, however, stood on Gallows Hill like a lighthouse. There appeared to be candles in every window. As the carriage shuddered to a halt at the thick foreboding door, the one passenger was spirited inside and down its narrow stone corridors to a small shuttered room at the back of the building, secured and safe from prying eyes.

The room was warm and crowded, there was an overpowering aroma of incense clouding the air. At least a dozen sisters in black stood about mumbling almost silently. The man in white made his way directly to a small, simple, wooden crib which stood in the centre of the room. The crib had no decoration, it was clearly not an object made by an excited parent awaiting the arrival of a precious child.

"Sister Prudence," he called, craning his head to see her whereabouts. The sister emerged from the ranks and grasped his hand, raising it to her lips.

"My Lord Keeper," she said.

"Are you sure she was alone?" he asked.

The woman was certain, a gardener who had worked at the convent for many years was on the hill when the tree fell. "He was on it in a matter of moments, hoping to catch squirrels or collect eggs from its fallen branches," she explained.

"So," he said, "there was no possibility another was removed before he arrived, or could he himself have removed another before he informed you?"

"None," she assured him. The gardener not only lived within the walls of the convent, but he had, in the past, been tasked with sensitive operations on behalf of the Brotherhood itself. Sister Prudence trusted him implicitly.

The Keeper thanked the Sister and her order for their diligence and asked them to leave the room. The man, now alone, looked at the child, who was, as far as he could tell, unremarkable in appearance. She seemed to be three months old, even though she was discovered only a day hence, and was sleeping serenely.

"My lord," came a voice from behind, causing him to turn with a start. Another man had entered the room, tiny in stature and clad in the reddest of robes.

"It is true then, they have sent…" he paused, "…it?"

"It would appear so," came the reply. The man in red circled the crib and extending a finger, poked the child with a pointed fingernail.

"Why a baby?" he finally asked.

"I have been wondering about that myself, I assume they think we will care for it, learning the value of parenting perhaps," he sneered. The man in red prodded the child once more and lowered his voice so it became cold and calculating. "We already know how to dispatch it. We should get rid of it quickly before it grows."

"Again, this is something I have considered, but if we do that, they will just send it again, and next time, we may not be as fortunate to discover it ourselves." The man in white crossed the room and closed the door. "Consider," he said, "I believe we have a unique opportunity to…" he seated himself on a nearby stool, "…to use this occurrence to our advantage."

"As long as this child is here," he continued, "we *should* protect it."

"After all," he continued, "we already know how to restrain them, and as you say, how to dispose of them."

The short man in red was listening silently, but suddenly became very animated, "I could further my research, and what better a subject to work with," his thoughts were racing ahead of him, "we could keep it here indefinitely."

"Yes, my friend," smiled the man in white. "Not only can we confound their plans, but more importantly," he raised a hand and the man in red helped him to his feet, then staring once more into the crib, said, "this child will make it possible to execute our own."

The Islands

On maps, the islands were shown as two primary landmasses. The first comprised Anglia in the south, and on its northern border were the Celtlands. To the west was a separate smaller island called Erin, and in the far north, there were several dozens of much smaller islands scattered in the northern sea.

The islands had known peace in one form or another for centuries. Its scattered towns and villages, pastoral by nature, hushed and ordered. Each region from the chalk cliffs on Anglia's southernmost coast, to the rugged grandeur of the isles in the north, ruled with even-handedness and cooperation. The heads of the free tribes welcomed each other's patronage in matters of trade and celebrated each other's distinctness.

The coastal fishermen at Appledore and those further to the west at Exe bartered with the Northumbrian cattle farmers. Shepherds from Trent would trade in harmony with the cider apple growers of Rochester; commerce aside, the people also came together to give thanks.

The solstices, winter and summer would see an enthusiastic migration to the island's most westerly tip, the home of the Brotherhood of the Celestial Majesty. The celebrations were stuff of legends. Highland games, wrestling, and rodeo. Singing, dancing, and carousing, colour, pageantry, and carnival.

Tented villages would appear overnight. Roaring campfires regaled with barely plausible tales of swaggering adventurers and miscreant ne'er do-wells. Ale would flow, hogs seasoned with sage and wild garlic, roasted. All the while music of fiddle and drum would weave through the scented smoke-filled air.

At sunrise, the white-robed Brotherhood, the religious mentors of the isles, would usher in the dawn and cultivate a more sombre and reverential mood, a brief moratorium in the revelries. Thanks would be given, neighbours embraced, and then after a minute of perfect silence observed by all, a cacophony, a celebratory explosion of noise, trumpet blasts, howls and wails, pots and pans being clattered, bedlam, a detonation loud enough to scare the bravest of demons back to Hades and beyond. This was the way of life for generations, kinship reigned.

The Brotherhood, however, over the years had transformed itself to be a dogmatic maker of rules and meddlers in lives. The transformation had been gradual. The clergy becoming more militant with the passing of each new edit, those who did not pay proper respect to the laws were forced from their land and left to starve. The land then given to those whose support was of more benefit to the Brotherhood. In return for their obedience and support, the people would receive guidance in all things celestial and mundane. The word of the gods delivered directly to the people. Protection for one's soul, and if required, a sword to protect everything else.

More than this, the most important thing to the farmers and sailors of the islands were the astonishingly accurate weather and fishing forecast. Nets could be cast with the guarantee of a bumper catch. Nobody lost crops to early frost or late snow. Barrels would be readied for the heaviest rains in order to deal with the coming summer droughts.

It was said that a rich apple grower was told the exact time lightning would strike a dead tree causing a fire and the total destruction of his orchard. He had his farmhands on watch and as the tree was struck, the fire was immediately extinguished without the loss of one tree. Information on all things was available, at a price. Many a cheating husband was caught red-handed and red-faced. Merchants could know with all certainty where pirates lay in wait for their ships. They could choose to avoid the perils of the privateers or arm their ships to the teeth and be ready to fight.

The Brotherhood, though, had become complacent. While they cemented their hold on power on the islands, war in the guise of commerce and religion had become commonplace beyond their shores. Millions starved as the powerful chose to forget their promises to the weak and poor.

Armies were being amassed in all corners of the world. Giant empires chose arguments with one another; land and ideologies became the currency of conflict. Human life was no longer valued. Those without were sent to fight each other with nothing to gain but an early grave. To the north of the islands, Scandic tribes, warring fear mongers driven by such greed had drawn up their plans, and in dragon-headed, steam-powered battle ships, sailed south to plunder and conquer.

The Emissary

"Bring her to me!" the order was simple. "I want to hear what she has to say, bring her to me now!" The old man, dressed ornately in white, slammed shut the large volume he had been reading, sending a soft booming echo around the wood-lined chamber in which he was seated.

Doors at the far end of the room facing him opened, and four men in white armour entered with a shabby manacled figure at their core. Grasped by the shoulders, the figure was pushed to the front of the group before the increasingly irritated figure in white.

The two gazed at one another for a while, the woman in irons surveyed the room, in which were seated a dozen men dressed in the same attire as the man glaring at her. The room was plain, but the walls were hung with ornate banners, whose meanings were lost to her.

The differences in the two could not be more apparent. Not just in the style of their dress, but their demeanours also. Rage from one, calm the other. The old man stood. "Well," he began. "I assume you did not come all this way to stand mute before me." He was about to continue but the woman interrupted.

"I did not come to stand before anyone," she said calmly, "I found myself here, as I have so many times before to…"

The older man erupted, almost leaping in the air, "Yes, just like before, to interfere, to meddle." The man in white leaned forward, smashing his gnarled fists on the desk in front of him. "We shall have no more of it!" he bellowed. "No more!"

The woman remained placid; her face betrayed no emotion. She raised her head and looked earnestly at the agitated man before her. "Have you ever tried to explain yourself to a dog?" she asked him.

If this question was intended to placate the man, it had the opposite effect. "Dogs are we now?" he bellowed.

The woman was unmoved and continued, "Your dog chases a bear, you beg for it to come to you, but it does not listen." Her voice began changing, switching from her voice to a male voice. It drifted from one direction then another, a single voice then a chorus, old and young, familiar then foreign.

"Stop with your trickery, woman!" the man screamed.

The woman, seemingly unaware, continued, "The beloved dog is badly injured, and as an act of kindness, you end its life." She was now staring directly at the man before her. "You can draw on all your knowledge, use all your words, try and explain, but the dog will never understand."

The man was now puce in the face, the veins in his neck and forehead appeared to be at bursting point. "Do you mean to put us down?" he hissed.

"No," said the woman calmly, "we are simply trying to keep you from the bear."

He inhaled deeply, "You have played with us for the last time," he gasped. "You say you want to keep us safe, when what you really want is us cowering at your heel and running when you whistle, well, we have our own plans," he said menacingly. He seated himself and leaned back in his chair, a slight nod to the guards and she was back in their grasp. "Take her below," he said with a wave of his hand. "Deal with her in the proscribed way," he stared at the unfortunate woman, "strap her to the Maiden," he growled. Then dragging himself to his feet, he added, "Send her back to where she came from."

The woman put up no fight, no struggle at all. She was vanished through the doors to be seen no more. An uneasy calm returned to the room. The old man said nothing for a full ten minutes then abruptly stood and left. Once in the hallway, the much smaller man, clad in red, joined him. The two of them strode along the dimly lit stone corridor and entered a much brighter room that overlooked the sea.

On a small stool by the window sat a woman with her face in her hands, softly sobbing. The two men were unconcerned. "What have you done?" asked the woman accusingly, "Where are my sisters?" She was about to continue her questioning when she gulped a sharp intake of breath; in her mind, she could see the flash of blades, feel a searing pain, and then nothing. She clutched her chest and glared at her captors. "Is this how it will be now?" she screamed. There was no anger in her eyes though, "It's not too late," she whimpered, "you can still change the path you have set yourselves on."

The man in white reached towards the seated woman. He grasped her by the chin and turned her face towards him. "Tell me what you see," he insisted.

The woman shook free of his grasp, 'I have told you before, I cannot see what happens in the ocean when I'm away from it any more than you can." The tall man rolled his eyes as if to mock her. She was unmoved by his petulant playacting and continued, "All raindrops eventually join the ocean," she said.

The man in white turned to his companion. "We ask questions, she answers with riddles," he scoffed.

She rose to her feet, becoming impatient, taking both men by surprise and making them step back from her. She could not suppress a wry smile at noticing their reservations. She was desperate to make them understand but was beginning to realise she might be wasting her breath. She inhaled and tried to find the words, "We are the ocean, and you are the rain."

She reached to the man in white and took his hand. "You do not try and join with us, instead you try and control us, manipulate us, master us." She released the man's hand and seated herself once more, then continued, "Until you understand that we are the same, you will always fail."

There was a moment of silence which was finally broken by the old man. He cleared his throat. "Let me be plain," he began, "I understand perfectly." He turned and began to walk away from her, while the smaller man produced two sets of chains, attaching one to her wrists, he then dropped to his knees and cuffed her ankles.

The older man turned as he approached the door having been joined by the man in red. He fixed the woman with a cold glare. "We will stay on our path, we will proceed with our plans, and you..." he raised his arm and pointed a bony finger at her, "...you will play your part."

The Rhyme and the Reason

When the moon is full,
when the sun is hot,
when the frost is raw,
and the dead, they rot.

They come to dance and *misdemean,*
they play their games,
to steal your dreams.
Beautiful faces hide devious hands.
Come from afar to rule our lands.

They mire your mind.
Your thoughts to souse.
You'll be led by the nose to the charnel house.

No more of this, we Brothers, now shall act!
In chains of iron, we bind this unholy pact.
To the Maiden shackled, we send them screaming,
our own world to rule
an end of their scheming.

Yet be forever on guard,
foretold is the final traitor,
the fire, pain, and judgement of,
the fearsome Desolator.

For when begin the end of days,
and the beast, it stalks our land,
with its name a' locked in a gilded cage,
our victory will be at hand.

So, apostates and heretics take heed!
for none are beyond our reach,
no difference if a God or man,
our lessons we will teach!

Our truth, our flag,
Now hear our caution well!
Take the vow and bend to us,
or we will damn you all to hell!

From the Second Book of Verse:
The Brotherhood of the Celestial Majesty

The Old Woman

The sun was rising, and the early morning clouds were carding through the tops of the pine forest. The smell of smoke hung stale in the air. Shards of light cast long dissolving shadows across the damp morning grass; as the old woman stepped from her shelter, she squinted, shielding her eyes from the young sun.

The scene was serene and beautiful, it transported her back to the time of her ancestors, who had hunted and farmed this land for countless generations; they saw no reason this would not continue. She thought back to when she was a child: the first time the travellers from other lands had arrived in ships, bringing the promise of trade, but instead, stole their lands, destroyed their beliefs and denied them their history and their future. Their innocence and friendship were repaid with avarice and cruelty.

The decades marched on as her people were corralled and slaughtered like animals or cut down by foreign disease. The young men killed in raids and the children herded together to be taught new ways of thinking by those who thought they knew better.

She saw her people reduced to a shadow of their former proud selves, now living in encampments on the borders of towns built on the land they used to call home. She watched as they turned to wine and violence, trying desperately to fit into the new world.

How long would it be, she thought, before all memory of her nation would be lost? When would be the last time her milky eyes would look upon a child born of her past? Who would be the last child she would tell stories of the old times, when the people and the land cared for one another?

The thoughts solidified in her mind, weighing her body down with the bitter pain of memory. She could see the old world and the new, she could feel both joy and pain, the hope and despair of all families, wherever they were in the world. The pain charged her with energy, it made her strong as when she was a young woman, and with the sting of tears in her eyes, she fell to her knees and forced her hands into the earth.

The Hill Tribes

The first landing and subsequent slaughter was at the township of York. The beaches at the Northern Sea, its idyllic hamlets overrun; men, women and children ruthlessly and efficiently put to the sword, and those who tried to flee were cut down in the sulphurous smoke of musket fire. No one had occasion to enquire as to the name of the Generals in command of the invaders, those who came asking were swiftly dispatched. Their legions swept west decimating all before them.

Those not butchered were shackled and herded to the invaders' ships. Their orders, to sail north to the salt mines and then further into the interior. The people of the islands turned to the Brotherhood for salvation, but none was forthcoming. The Brotherhood had fled and abandoned its flock.

Into the second week of the raids, the burning horizon bled smoke to the bruised sky. The acrid stench of burned livestock and crops painted the storm clouds purple and black, it was as if the Desolator had taken residence in the lands and all was lost.

A mandate was sent to all the corners of the islands, the invaders now claimed these lands and the double-headed dragon flag would fly there for evermore. All townships, villages and hamlets were to send one-tenth of all their populations to the long ships for transportation. Those who resisted would die on the gallows.

The trek of the defeated began; farmers, smithies, teachers and doctors, none were spared. The invaders' victory was seemingly complete, as in chains, the spoils of war accepted their fate.

It had been twenty-two days since the raids had begun. Beaches the length and breadth of the islands now resembled cattle markets. In pens, the slaves were separated by sex, then age and occupation. Bureaucrats filed and sorted their human chattels. One such accountant reached an enclosure where the dunes met the forest. Within it was one person cloaked from head to foot, kneeling silently as if at prayer.

"You stand!" barked the club-wielding functionary. With no movement evident from the individual, he thumped him on the shoulder as if to rouse him from sleep. "If you are not dead, you soon will be, now stand when you are ordered!"

The hooded figure straightened slightly and began to rise, casting an enormous shadow over the man standing on the sand in front of him. Slowly, he pushed the hood back from his head, revealing a blue-painted face with sparkling black eyes. A smile danced across blood red lips. What was clearly a giant of a man leaned closer as if to inspect the much smaller and noticeably shaken individual with the club. "I bring you greetings from my people," he began, "I am Fuldus of The Hill Tribes, and I am the only person this day who will offer you a smile."

A crowd had begun to gather and standing before him now were some ten to a dozen heavily armed raiders. "I'll not only offer you a smile but some advice also, return to your ships and be on your way." The raiders could not believe their ears and laughed aloud at the suggestion. Fuldus roared with them, like old friends sharing a joke. "Be on your way, and we will say no more about it, less said soonest mended." The laughter grew, as did the crowd. Fuldus, however, had ceased to look amused.

He raised his hand and pulled at the gold cord fastening his cloak, and with his other hand, he produced a curved, furrowed horn. "I also bring you a gift." The curious raiders were crowding closer to catch a glimpse of what was being held. Fuldus raised it high so all could see. "This," he began, loud enough for them to hear, "is a trumpet made from an animal I killed just this very morning, and as I watched the life gush from its veins, I thought to myself how satisfying it will be to watch you all die in the same way."

The horn was at Fuldus' lips in a flash and the blast from it took all by surprise, except those who had been waiting for it. His cloak slipped from his shoulders to reveal an armoured chest plate, as a terrible howling rose from the forest. More trumpet blasts were met with drumming and screaming. All faces turned to the forest; its trembling trees, the splintering of branches and bracken under foot, spoke of the yet unseen onrushing advance.

Then lurching from the foliage's cover came monstrous apparitions flanked by enormous howling and baying dogs. Men and women as big as and some bigger than the one who had been so entertaining only moments earlier. Painted bodies and faces, metal-armoured, decorated with bone and skull, hurtling towards the now panicking and scattering raiders.

Fuldus stood, surrounded, the crowd now scrabbling for their weapons, desperate to protect themselves. He had no such problem, grasping his sword, hidden until now by his cloak; he leapt at those around him. The sword's blade, double-edged and almost six feet in length, quickly found its mark. Two raiders fell immediately, one headless. Slashing and swinging, he cleared a space in which to work, and dispatched another half-dozen.

The howling masses swept down through the crowded beach, hacking and chopping as they went. The small band, though vastly outnumbered, soon had the raiders running to the shore and the safety of the long boats. Severed limbs, blood-stained sands and shattered bodies bore testament to the savage ferocity of Fuldus and his tribe. In less than an hour, the rout was complete; six-hundred Scandinavians were dead. Fuldus had lost only two from sixty-eight of his kin.

Kneeling now before Fuldus was General Klimt, the leader of the seemingly invincible force from the sea. A man of no more than thirty years and not as experienced in warfare as he had first thought. The pain of defeat was etched on his face. His head bowed awaiting his fate. Fuldus was seated on an up-turned coracle, decorated with the shields and helmets of the conquered, "Do not cower before me, General, your army, after all, fought well against the unarmed and the weak." Mocking laughter rippled through the assembled crowds of warriors and, now, free men.

Fuldus stood, "As a soldier, you were found wanting, as a man, you should be ashamed." Striding forwards, he raised his sword above his head. "You do not even deserve death," he hissed, "but I am merciful and shall gift it to you regardless of your failings." Fuldus positioned himself as two of kin grasped the general's shoulders and dragged him to his feet. "You shall not die on your knees," he announced, "you see my mercy knows no bounds."

The ram's horns rent the air once more as Fuldus steadied himself, but just before he could strike, the shrieking voice of a young boy begging stayed the execution. "Sir!" the boy burst from the crowd and threw himself at his feet. "Sir," he repeated, "please don't kill my pa. I've got four sisters and a mother. They will starve. Take my life instead and send him home, banish him, sir, but please spare him." Fuldus lowered his weapon, its tip sinking into the sand until it stood upright by itself.

Reaching down, he took the boy by the scruff of his neck, lifting him until their eyes met. The blonde child was gaunt and sickly looking, but with striking sapphire blue eyes, he looked no more than ten years old. His tears on the verge of falling but valiantly under control. A broad smile swept across Fuldus' mouth, then narrowing his eyes and careful not to lose the boy's gaze, he lowered him to his feet, so he was standing upright. The boy pushed back his shoulders and stood to his best attention. Fuldus' gaze now lighted upon Klimt, "General, it would appear there is some honour and gallantry in your family line after all, should I take your heroic son's offer?" Klimt dropped to his knees once more, horror in his wide eyes not knowing if the barbarian who had led the slaughter of his garrison would willingly execute a child in his stead.

"For the love of the gods, sir, no!" he cried.

Fuldus lunged towards the terrified general, and grasping his throat, pulled the man towards him. Their faces touched, Klimt could feel hot sour breath on his lips, and through his clenched teeth, Fuldus growlingly whispered, "Do not talk to me of the gods, I shall be dealing with their representatives shortly." He hurled the general to the sand and returned his gaze to the now petrified child. "What is your name, boy?" he barked.

The boy's mouth moved but nothing was forthcoming, he swallowed hard. "Kristan, sir," came the eventual reply.

Fuldus, without looking, retrieved his sword, and with its point raised to the general's chin, "Say goodbye to your father, Kristan." The gleaming blade sliced through the air and ended the life of General Klimt.

His death was met only with the stifled sobs of his son. He raised his head, hatred burning in his eyes; he sprang towards the giant before him, fists flying and shrieking like a banshee. Fuldus opened his huge hand and swatted the boy to one side, drawing blood from his nose.

"Save your anger for the fools who sent you here, boy," the tone in his voice was almost soothing. As he turned to walk away, the boy was already being pulled to his feet.

"My Lord Fuldus," came a voice, Fuldus stopped.

"What should we do with the boy?" asked one of his men.

Fuldus paused for a moment and considered his answer carefully. *Mercy or ruthlessness,* he thought, he had enough horrors haunting his sleep without staining his hands with the blood of a child. He was still quite fond of sleeping, even if it was only in fits and starts. He turned and looked at the boy, who now seemed half the size he was before. "Find a crew, give them a ship, round up the wounded and send them back to their home with the boy." He found himself once again face to face with the child. "Go home, care for your mother and sisters. Remember this simple act of kindness, Kristan." He began to stride away, and without turning, he raised his voice loud enough for all to hear, "But be sure to tell your masters never to try their luck here again, mercy does not come naturally to me."

The Lizard

The next three days were spent camped at the victory site. Riders were arriving every few hours, telling of similar victories across the island: equally savage in efficiency and as lenient in losses. Those of the tribes who had fallen were honoured, a funeral pyre built, and the bodies cremated. Tribesmen were never buried; they blazed their way to the next world. 'From the earth to the sky' was the blessing that sent them on their way to whatever lay beyond.

With the riders came a catalogue of the spoils of war. In total, the tribes had captured sixteen steamships, twelve steam waggons, hundreds of muskets and barrels of gunpowder. The steam engine had been in use on the islands for many decades, for farming and such mundane applications, but never had it been so effectively used as to power the machines of war.

Fuldus was hypnotised by the sheer delicious deviance of it. *A combine harvester,* he thought, *that can kill as effectively as the plague.* He could see the future unfurling before him. He and his kin had saved the people and it was their rightful place to see they remained safe. None of the other tribes would be equipped to oppose him, decimated as they were from the initial attacks. He would, however, need to negotiate with the Brotherhood, and as he expected, they returned from hiding at sunrise the very next day.

The head of the order, the rather pompously titled Keeper of the Secrets, was aged somewhere between sixty and hundred years, no one was sure. By all accounts, he was humourless and ill tempered, his power over the people, however, was ironclad. His use of ritual and apparent knowledge of the inner workings of the universe gave him the air of a man in personal contact with the gods, it made him appear otherworldly and consequently invincible. Fuldus knew of him, but they had never met, and no one was entirely sure of his actual identity.

The Brotherhood had grown in number from a dozen or so when the order was founded to hundreds in every region. Aside from its ritual duties, they would collect tributes, not taxes, to fund the bloated position they now held. Tributes in form of food and livestock from smaller villages and townships, gold and precious stones from those with wealth and an appetite for power.

Through the forest, that had served Fuldus and his men so well as cover for their attack on the beaches just days before, now came a solemn procession of white-robed men carrying elegantly embroidered banners bearing the rising sun symbol of the Brotherhood. Each of the sun's beams was tipped with a different sign of the zodiac. The ornate banners fluttering in the cool sea breeze that carried with it the drumbeats and soft chanting of their approach.

The column had still not cleared the trees when those at its head had reached the beach. Fuldus was standing in the entrance of his yurt, which now doubled as his campaign headquarters. The procession began to fan out as it reached him. They formed orderly ranks in front of the faded red canvas of the tent, leaving a wide pathway between them. Still from the forest they came, some carrying flaming torches, others swinging ornate censers with clouds of sweet incense billowing from them.

Then finally, heavily armed soldiers, still clad in white but armoured and gleaming, and a sedan chair held aloft by sixteen men, four at each corner. The chair, intricate and stately, swayed through the clearing left by those at the head of the procession. Finally, the chair reached where Fuldus was standing surrounded by his own warriors. He could not help but notice how simple the robes of the Brothers were, and how stark the contrast was to the mobile throne and its occupant. The legs of the chair were serpentine, their tails coiled to make round feet. Their bodies rising upright as legs, their heads flattened to support a plush, dark, burgundy leather cushion.

The back of the chair rose in four sections, each carved with scenes depicting one of the four seasons: a meadow in spring, the blazing summer sun, the fruits of the autumn harvest and the snows of winter. In the centre of the four friezes was a single piece of amber about the size of a dinner plate, cut like the finest diamond so the light splintered through it and painted those around it.

The light, however, fell predominantly on the one seated in the chair, now leaning forwards with one elbow on his knee, the other hand outstretched towards Fuldus, who obligingly took it and helped him to step down onto the sands. He drew a breath and straightened his frame, obviously stiff from the journey. Fuldus momentarily winced at the sound of creaking coming from the man's joints and sinews. He was dressed head to foot in white, and as he prepared himself to speak, all others in his party dropped to one knee. Fuldus cast his eyes towards his own kin, and they echoed the action.

The only two standing now were Fuldus and the Keeper of the Secrets himself. He inhaled long and deep through his nostrils, then clearing his throat, began, "I offer the blessings of the Brotherhood on you and your men; I assume I am addressing the formidable Fuldus." Fuldus gave a polite bow and smiled. The old man continued, "Myself, my Brothers, and the peoples of these islands are in the debt of you and your brave kin." He cast his head slowly from side to side in acknowledgement of the men and women around him, whilst also taking an estimate of their numbers. "I ask you, Fuldus, to travel west with me to Lizard Island, where you will be treated in the manner a lord such as yourself truly deserves. You will join me, yes." He sucked air through his dry lips. "I will accept no refusal," he said with the thinnest of smiles, the insistence in his voice was obvious.

Knowing Fuldus and his hoard must be handled with the utmost respect and diplomacy, he did, however, allow Fuldus no time to respond. The man with the wheezing voice and calm polite demeanour, this time unaided, seated himself once more and as he did so, all those around him sprang to their feet. Fuldus could not help but be amused by this spectacle, apparently string-less puppets reacting to their master's orchestration.

Now once more comfortable in his seat, he continued, "My friend, pack whatever you need for our two-day journey west, your comfort is of the utmost importance to me." An obsequious smile parted his lips, slowly revealing his yellowing teeth, each alternately studded with a ruby and an emerald.

The sight momentarily threw Fuldus, but he quickly composed himself and taking a step forward, he said with faux humility, "Your eminence is too kind, my men and encampment are at your disposal. Allow me one hour, if you will, so I might leave orders with my commanders for the continued protection of these islands, and I will of course gladly travel with you." Fuldus bowed a deep and courteous bow, and without raising himself fully upright, receded until he was cloistered in his tent. Half a dozen helmeted, and armoured giants followed behind.

The tent was strewn with cushions of various colours, sizes and fabrics. In a clear space at the centre of the floor, lay maps and charts. Fuldus kicked his way through them and sat on a large stool, which groaned as he settled. He took a long gulp of water from a heavy ornate glass which was sitting nearby. When it was drained, he hurled it to the floor. He could barely contain his rage, his emotions and muscles fighting each other for control of his body and facial expressions.

He pulled a bone-handled dagger from his belt, the silver blade, narrow and plain, had remained unused until this point in its existence. Fuldus drew the blade across the palm of his hand, the cold sting followed by the warm sticky flow of his own blood finally calmed him enough so he could speak. In not much more than a throaty whisper, he looked to his men, "I knew he would come, that pious, odious, malicious, pompous…" struggling to keep himself in check once more he forced his fist into his mouth and bit down.

Sarn, Fuldus' cousin and second in command, placed his hand on his shoulder. "Save your rage, Fuldus, the time for revenge is at hand, my friend."

Fuldus looked at him, calm returning to his being. He clasped his cousin in a bear hug, squeezing the air from his lungs, "Revenge is a sweet word, but I do not see this as revenge." He re-sheathed his dagger, and now composed said, "Revenge can be a misguided enterprise, full of hate and childish petulance, revenge is not what this is. This is retribution."

A warrior child of about fourteen years of age, and small for one of his kind, scurried towards Fuldus with a roughly hewn wooden bowl containing steaming water and began to cleanse and dress the wound to his hand. Fuldus smiled at the boy and ushered him away, then changing his mind, he beckoned, "Young warrior, wait, are you truly ready to serve with me?"

The lad straightened as tall as he could, "My Lord Fuldus, I am ready to die with you," and at that, he dropped to one knee.

Fuldus reached down and ruffled his hair, "Let's hope it does not come to that," he smiled.

Then turning to Sarn, he said quietly, "Give me a three-hour head start, I am guessing a column this strong in numbers will stick to the coastal paths. You and three dozen of our stealthiest, make your way west through the forests. Have another dozen or so follow on the road. When you arrive, you will find a warm welcome waiting for you. Remember, my Brothers, we do this for all the fallen, now leave me and this young warrior alone."

Minutes later, Fuldus emerged from the tent carrying a wicker basket. Three white-robed attendants approached him. Two of them relieved him of his belongings, placing them carefully on an open-backed supply cart. With that, the other helped Fuldus mount his horse and take his place in the procession just behind the Keeper's chair.

As the parade left the beaches, the sun had barely cleared the tallest trees, but the temperature had already risen to an uncomfortable level. Clouds of mosquitoes filled the air, irritating people and animals alike. As Fuldus had reasoned, the entourage elected to follow the path which hugged the shoreline west to Lizard Island.

The choice of the island as the Brotherhood's spiritual home was as much strategic as it was guided by any sense of a higher calling. The island was formed roughly twenty years previous during a storm of such ferocity; tales of it had become legend and recounted whenever a high wind blew. Sixteen fishermen from Hellston lost their lives that night. Mountainous waves for hours battered a slender isthmus, until it gave way at its narrowest point and the island was formed at its most westerly tip. The newly formed Lizard Island was now only accessible by a heavily guarded bridge built by the Brotherhood, and there stood the Chapel of Secrets.

The Chapel was a fabulously intricate white structure of spires and domes that gleamed and shimmered in the sun and became almost invisible when its white rays bounced off the sea. When the mists would roll in from the ocean, ghostlike and shrouded it stood, spectral and mysterious. The entire building appeared to be constructed of stone, marble, or alabaster, but it was so highly polished it was impossible to tell.

Double doors fronted the one entrance to the inner sanctum of the Chapel of Secrets. Some forty feet in height, they were emblazoned with the same rising sun emblems as those on the processional banners. Like everything else, they were smooth as glass. The bridge across was just wide enough for the Keeper of the Secrets' sedan chair to be carried, or a single file of medium-sized waggons to squeeze deftly through.

Locals told stories of how privateers from the south, dreaming of rich plunder, had set sail with six frigates. Four were lost to the rocks, which were only visible if the sea decided to be kind. The two ships, which got close enough to the polished walls, found no purchase for their grappling hooks, or indeed any way to climb by hand.

Dejected, they turned to set sail for home. Some said the Keeper, so incensed by the audacity of the attempted felony, stood atop the tallest spire and summoned the spirits of the deep to swallow the ships and their unfortunate occupants as a warning to any others who might be so foolhardy.

The more grounded amongst those who tell the story, talk of small invisible windows sliding open and a volley of canon fire splintering the hulls of the retreating pirate ships, sending their crew's smoking bodies to the seabed. Whichever version of the tale you choose to believe, no one had since tried to enter the Chapel uninvited.

Fuldus was lost in thought as the Brotherhood slowly continued towards home. Astride his horse—which was a massive beast, the largest shire horse to be found in the district, and which was certainly not built for speed or comfort—a dull ache and soreness were beginning to creep through the big man's muscles. The heat had risen to the extreme for the time of year, and he had lost count of the number of midges that had feasted on his blood.

After five hours of continuous riding, the file of weary brethren stopped to rest at a clearing and take on water and a light luncheon of dried beef and fresh fruit. Fuldus used the time to count the numbers in the party. One Keeper, sixteen lackeys, forty assorted flag bearers, nearly sixty in the white-robed choir, who had not ceased their incantations since leaving the beach, and thirty heavily armed infantrymen. He could not help but admire the control the Keeper of the Secrets had over such numbers, but any time his mind formed a notion of admiration for the man, he would bite his tongue and remind himself of his true feelings.

The cortege had rested for barely a quarter of an hour before they were on the move again. For the entire length of the journey so far, the Keeper had not been seen. Secluded now as he was by a bleached-white damask and gold-fringed curtain that averted all prying eyes.

Fuldus held this man directly responsible for the ignorance of most of his subjects to the world beyond Anglia. An ignorance for which they had paid dearly in the previous weeks. He wondered what the islands would be like if the power of knowledge, steam and commerce had taken control, rather than the piety of the Brotherhood. Never again would these lands that he held so dear be a soft target for greedy mercenaries.

His travelling companions, without exception, had not disturbed him thus far, and he was beginning to miss the camaraderie of his own company. Onwards the journey went until the summer sun began to set and the road was considered too dangerous to travel by torch light. A camp was hastily erected. The occupant of the sedan chair was again notable by his absence.

The sounds of the summer night crept in with the cooling air, which came as such a relief after the heat of the day. Roosting crows, cawing home their own kind. Black wings in a pale blue sky, heralding the dark. The call of an owl was the only thing Fuldus was aware of as he crawled into the tent provided for him. He slept fleetingly, but dreamed regardless: fevered boyhood dreams, dreams of running, panic and fear haunted the clouds of his spirit.

Try as he might, he could not stop the ghosts of a sixteen strong hunting party, their bravado dissolving into the distance with the thunderous rain. Fuldus would find himself standing alone being soaked by the downpour, watching as a young boy, slowly pulled himself from his thorny hiding place and raced across the swollen river to the fallen bodies of his parents. Hoof-shaped puddles mingled with hair, blood and tears, where moments before a mighty warrior begged for the life of his wife and child, but to no avail. The woman and her daughter butchered, and the man dying.

Barely holding back his tears of frustration and anger, Fuldus and the boy would drop to their knees and tenderly kiss their mother and sister goodbye. All they could do was look on as they were taken from them. The boy swallowed his sobs, knowing very well the hunting party was not that far away and he was still in very real danger. *How bad could it be?* he thought. *He could be with his family if they did come back and find him, he would welcome the site of their white armour.*

Through tears, he would watch the boy return to his father. "Pa, Pa," he whispered, his frantic pleas going unanswered. The boy pounding on the big man's chest, not caring now if his cries could be heard. There was nothing from his father. Defeated, he sank his face into his blood and rain-soaked chest and screamed in unison with the thunder.

A choking cough snapped the boy back into the moment. The big man's eyes opening slowly, but not fully. He swallowed hard but could not stem the flow of blood into his mouth. "Pa!" screamed the boy, almost giddy trying to pull his father to his feet. "We can make it back to the caves from here, or shall I go for help?"

The man opened his eyes wider, a smile on his lips. "Son, go, save yourself," his eyelids flickered as he fought the pain racking his body, and placing his fingers gently on the boy's mouth to stop him from speaking, continued, "Become strong, be patient and when the time is right..." he gulped down air, determined to finish what he was saying, "When the time is right—find those who have done these wicked things—" he pulled the boy's ear close to his lips and whispered, "wreak havoc."

In the morning, the cold sweats of the previous night were gone, but the instruction as always remained with him.

After Fuldus had dressed, a silent attendant entered his tent holding a cup of honeyed-nettle tea, warm soda bread and some salty chunks of strong cheddar. A large bowl and a piece of rough white linen had been left just in sight of the tent entrance. Fuldus took this as an invitation to refresh himself. No sooner had he done this, and the column moved onwards accompanied by the now grating monotone chants of his companions.

"I trust you slept well, my friend," came a voice from inside the tented sedan chair. "You must forgive me for my continued seclusion, it is just an old man's indulgence and an intolerance of the sun, please take no offence."

Fuldus assured his invisible companion that that was the case, and for the remains of the day, he heard not another word spoken.

The Brotherhood's path west took them through very few settlements. Those, however, they did come across displayed the same behaviour. No one was to be seen, but offerings of bread, fruit, mead and wine were left by the roadside. Everything was collected and thrown into baskets on the back of the wagon where Fuldus' own belongings were also stowed.

The camp the second night was much the same as the one before. Silent and sombre with no sense of joy. The islands after all had just been delivered from the hands of invaders. Surely this was cause for some celebration. The camp regardless remained undisturbed. Fuldus again found himself alone in his tent. Just as he was closing his eyes in hope of a dreamless sleep, a voice startled him back to the land of the living.

"My lord," the hushed voice was coming from behind the tent. Fuldus could see nothing of who was talking, a young voice eager and excited continued. "My Lord Fuldus, I have secured the robes. I am ready, my lord, and I will not fail you."

With that, the tent returned to silence. Not even the muffled sounds from outside, the soft billow of flags in the night breeze and the cry of a fox, eerie and anguished, like a baby calling for its mother were going to disturb Fuldus now. He made himself comfortable, stretched himself out and fell soundly asleep.

After the same drab routine as the previous day, it was only another three hours and the return to Lizard Island was at hand. Trumpet blasts now dramatically ended the silence. The road to the Chapel was completely barren, partially because of the hostile salt wind that blasted the landscape, but also anything which could hinder the view of the approach road from the watchtowers had been removed. The building was truly impressive, Fuldus almost gasped when he first took it in.

The day was clear and warm, heat shimmered on the outer walls and domes. Oasis-like, it looked as if it would disappear as soon as one might try to enter. The sense of relief was palpable from the parading Brothers, home at last. The trumpet calls continued until the tail end of the column was inside the previously hidden courtyard, and the mighty doors firmly secured. No sooner had those returning heard them slam, they were gone vanishing into countless smaller doorways on all sides leading to Fuldus knew not where.

Silence again returned, the sedan chair was lowered, silently and softly onto the polished floor. Wooden steps were unfolded, and the ghost-like old man was helped down them. Fuldus was beckoned to dismount and obliged instantly. His horse was led away to be groomed, watered and fed.

Directly opposite the great entrance doors were another pair of doors exact in every detail, except they were roughly half the size. The Keeper, whose robes hid his feet, appeared to float towards Fuldus and grasping him by the elbow, they both turned towards them as they opened as if by magic. Upon entering Fuldus found himself in a finely furnished, but window-less room. The doors closed again, not by magic, but by two burly guards.

"Please, my friend," the old man waved his hand around in the air, as if to say look around you, "Please make yourself comfortable, rest a while." The Keeper stepped away from Fuldus but continued to speak, "We shall dine after we have both recovered, there is much to discuss of the future."

Another smaller door opened to the left of the room; a flickering light spilled out onto the floor as the Keeper disappeared through it with the two guards in close pursuit. The sound of the door snapping closed echoed between the smooth walls and Fuldus found himself alone. Clean clothes had been delivered to him, fresh fruit, meat and wine also. Then a golden bathtub on wheels was rolled in, steaming and inviting. Fuldus, without any sense of humility, quickly undressed and soaked his aching body. After three days on the road, he had begun to find his own aroma quite offensive.

The hot scented waters were a welcome treat. As he bathed, his fresh clothes were laid out on the bed. Fuldus had barely even noticed it when he had first walked into the room. It looked a little small for his frame, but it would do. After drying himself, dressing and eating a small amount of fruit, he lay down on the feather-soft mattress and was soon dreaming of nothing.

He awoke slowly with no concept of the time. The room offered no clues as to the position of the sun or moon. There was the ever-present sound of chanting, but muffled and distant. Fuldus had indeed slept well and was now ready to deal with the Keeper and his vision of the future.

A gently ringing of a bell heralded the entrance to the room of a small man dressed differently from anyone Fuldus had ever encountered before. Firstly, and unlike everyone else in the Chapel, he was not dressed in white; his cloak, with its hood down, was of the deepest sinister red. The cloth not simple but rich and velvety, it hung around him like butchered meat. The man's hands were bedecked with jewellery. Rings of silver and gold on each finger, including the thumb. His nails were long and polished, shaped to a point. Fuldus closely studied the man's face, he was completely bald with no facial hair at all. No eyebrows, no eyelashes and certainly no beard nor moustache.

He was short and stood about five-feet tall, Fuldus, like many of his kin, were over seven feet in height and this made this oddly dressed fellow look even more diminutive. Perched on his thin nose was a pair of very dainty spectacles, which were attached to only one ear by a fine chain of gold.

He looked at Fuldus up and down and gave an unnecessarily deep and long bow. When upright, after what seemed like an eternity, he finally spoke. "I am, I assume, addressing Fuldus, commander of tribes and saviour of Anglia." Fuldus could not contain his amusement at this bizarre little man, and after checking there were no other seven-feet-tall warriors in the room with whom he could be confused, suppressed his laughter and nodded to confirm his identity. "I am the Keeper of the Laws," the man in red continued. "Before we enter the chamber of the Keeper of the Secrets, we must cleanse ourselves spiritually," sensing the big man's discomfort at this request, he quickly added, "It is our custom and very simple."

Fuldus' amusement was now replaced with dismay. "How," he enquired, "does one do this?"

The Keeper of the Laws produced from his sleeve a small bell and guided Fuldus to a large carved chair. "Please, my lord, be seated and we shall begin." Fuldus reluctantly obliged, making himself as comfortable as possible, and so the cleansing began. "Please close your eyes and listen only to the sound of my voice," was the only instruction he received.

A small bell began a rhythmic chiming, like a pin striking the eardrum. Hushed spoken words, barely audible. As hard as Fuldus tried, he could not understand what the man was mumbling. His mind was filling with water. The words were flooding his senses. Breathing became a chore. His body floating, lips moving. Slowly it was becoming clearer, but then it was gone. Only to return once more. Dreamlike confusion pulling him under, "…protect…protector…protector…protect her," was being repeated, again and again. He was drowning, try as he might, he could not find the surface, he wanted to rise and suck in air and breathe again. The liquid rays of the sun or moon were being pulled apart by the swirling water above him as he continued to sink toward darkness. The bell continued to chime, as did the murmurings. "Protector, protector, protect her." The words spiralled and danced through and around him. The chiming became a continuous metallic hum, "Protector, protect her, protector."

Fuldus found himself speaking but was not sure of what he was saying, when finally, aloud he yelled, "…and make your enemies family!"

He leapt from the chair, not used to his actions being beyond his control. He was unsteady on his feet and waded across the floor placing one hand on the wall to help regain his balance and senses. He turned accusingly to the Keeper of the Laws, fire in his eyes and teeth locked. "You get out of here!" he roared, his rage in vain, disbelief replacing it. He was alone, even the words were gone.

At that very moment, the door to the room opened and the servant who had brought in the bathtub and fresh clothes entered once more. Fuldus leapt at him pinning him to the wall lifting his feet from the floor. "Where did the red dwarf go?" he bellowed. Staring into the servants terrified eyes, he released him, stepping back, fists clenched snorting like a bull about to charge.

The unsuspecting man fell in a crumpled heap but instantly clambered to his knees in fear of his life, gasping for breath. "My lord, I saw no one," he spluttered. Fuldus stepped over him into the courtyard, but before he had time to speak, a rapturous burst of applause greeted him. The courtyard had been transformed into a banqueting hall.

A huge circular table had been placed, where seemingly moments before there was only silence and the cold floor. The warm glow of flickering candles gave the white walls a golden hue. Around the table were seated a variety of robed Brothers and others in civilian finery. Upon seeing Fuldus, all rose to their feet and began chanting his name, some pounding the table with their fists. The Keeper of the Secrets let this continue for a minute or so before raising his hand allowing order to take charge of the room once more. The Keeper was dressed as before in white, but his robes on this occasion were ornate, embroidered with gold thread and set with sapphires and emeralds at the cuffs and neckline.

The Keeper of the Secrets rose to his feet. "Fuldus, gathered here, in your honour are the lords of all the tribes from the four corners of these islands." He turned from left to right, "Celtic lords from the North and West. Chiefs of the moors and dales. The High Sheriff of the South. All here to salute you and your kin." Fuldus' head was reeling still, moments before he was ready to kill, now he was not sure what had even happened to him. He tried to look statesman-like to feel at home in such lofty company.

He inhaled deeply and composed himself, "Thank you, Brothers and lords alike, long have my people looked on your tribes and longed for your acceptance." Again, applause filled the room.

"Fuldus, be seated at my right hand," beckoned the Keeper. Fuldus duly obliged, and the feasting began. The large oak table groaned under the weight of the excessive fare before him: roasted swan, goose and duck, suckling pig and wild boar, pitchers of ale and wine, cheeses and breads, fruits, the likes of which he had never seen before. But to hide his ignorance, he kept his own secret.

Musicians had entered the courtyard and had taken up position in the table's core. Lively fiddle songs were played with verve and gusto. *So, unlike the sombre chants of the Brotherhood on the journey here,* Fuldus thought.

The transformation was miraculous. Where there was sobriety, now was revelry. Piety replaced with profanity. Fuldus surveyed those around him, the lords of the tribes. Which would be his ally, he wondered. Which of these sycophants of the Brotherhood would stand with him to bring the islands from the dark ages? If he had his way, their rule was soon to end, on whom other than his own kin could he rely.

Fuldus was aware of the many eyes on him. He could feel their wary stares, long had the tribesmen been feared and hunted, feared for their longevity and strength, savagely hunted for the same reasons. Their numbers though were a mystery, but there were obviously enough of them to rout the Scandinavian invaders.

Fuldus and his kin were now occupying every territory. Their victory complete, did they intend to return to the hills and forests? Would they live side by side with the other tribes? Would they return to seclusion? Or were they harbouring grudges? So very little was known of them. In times past, the Brotherhood had put a bounty on the heads of any of them, man, woman, or child, found where they were not welcome. Others had led raiding parties into the hills for sport. How Fuldus remembered those times, and he had not forgiven. Were they wondering if his tribes could be trusted now that their numbers had recovered to such a ferocious force?

The Keeper turned his head to Fuldus. "I am soon to retire to prayer, to thank the gods for aiding us in our dark time. We have much to discuss, your future, the future of your people and their safe return to the hills. In the morning, we will discuss many things."

With that, the Keeper began to rise but found himself unable to stand. Fuldus had grasped him by the wrist and pulled him back into his seat. The Keeper glared as him, "I will let your ignorance of etiquette allow you to lay hands on my person, this once, no man has the right…"

Before he could finish his gentle chastisement, Fuldus leaned in close, "Don't talk to me of rights, old man."

The room suddenly fell silent. Fuldus, trembling with rage, was standing in a flash. "You and your cronies have become fat and lazy. You allowed foreigners to walk in here and kill your families and take your lands, not to mention your dignity. What rights have you to sit here and feast, when the blood of my kin has saved you all!"

Many of the party were now on their feet and hurling abuse at him. How dare a tribesman address them with such rudeness and discourtesy?

"Silence yourself!" screamed the representative of the Northern Celts. Fuldus turned and picking up a carving knife, hurled it in his direction, narrowly missing the man's ear but embedding it in the back of his chair. At this, Fuldus stepped up onto the table. He glared down at the Keeper. "You want to discuss the future, let me tell you of the future, one that is not governed by you and your corrupt cohorts, on the whim of your gods."

The old man now free of Fuldus, stood and pointed a sinuous finger at the ranting giant, "Blasphemy, outrageous blasphemy, how dare you!" The Keeper retreated further from Fuldus, until he was against the wall, a curtain of red behind him silhouetting his frame. "This will not be tolerated, seize him!"

A sudden onrush of bodies engulfed Fuldus, sending him crashing to the ground in a tangle of limbs. With as much strength as he could muster, he erupted. Bodies flew in all directions, he was free, but unarmed.

Mallet-like fist rained down on anyone foolish enough to be near him, a side door into the courtyard opened and in flowed a dozen of the Brotherhood's troops armed with crossbows. A bolt flew and found its mark. Fuldus reeled back, tearing the shaft and tip from his shoulder.

"Hold your fire!" came the order from the Keeper. "No blood shed within the walls of the Chapel; it is the law." The guards remained tense and ready to fire, but all obeyed.

Fuldus knew when to play for time, an opportunity would surely arise. "You barbarian," the insult was spat at Fuldus by a paler than usual Keeper. "Did you think you could walk in here and change centuries of tradition to suit your own ends and that of the curs you call kin?" Fuldus could no longer feel the pain burning in his shoulder, rage was dulling it. "The Brotherhood knew your people were not to be trusted, we should have continued our purge until you were all but extinct."

Fuldus' eyes fixed on the older man, "A mistake to be sure, my lord, you had your chance, and a second will not come." A broad smile had returned to his lips.

The Keeper was incredulous. "Look at you, a smiling halfwit. It is your people who will receive no second chances. With you dead, your tribes will run for the hills and I shall personally see to it that not one of them is alive at the passing of this year."

The Keeper gestured to stairs which he knew led up to the Chapel's battlements. "The rocks and the ocean, Fuldus, that is the future that awaits you." The Keeper gestured and the guards grabbed Fuldus, pushing him towards the doorway. As the occupants of the room began to file into the stairwell, unnoticed a figure in white had made his way to the ornate gates which separated the banquet from the world outside.

The rapid clicking of oiled latches and cogs, the squealing of hinges and the cold chill of opening doors: The Chapel was unlocked. The Keeper spun on his heel, and upon seeing the man's white robes, he squealed,

"Brother, secure those doors immediately!" The cloaked figure, however, was gone. The pale light from the outside world trickled into the Chapel. "Coward!" he spluttered, assuming it to be a fleeing Brother. The figure in white had fulfilled his role, Fuldus watched as the young man who had vowed to serve him vanished from sight.

The courtyard was once again a cauldron of activity, ranks of infantry were streaming in from all sides to aid with the removal of Fuldus. One guard dashed to make the gates secure but was felled as a spinning axe hurled unseen buried itself in his skull. The soldiers in white immediately turned their attention to whatever might follow it.

Fuldus, in the confusion, was now free from his captors and was hurling any member of the Brotherhood in his path to the floor, so he could be free to join the oncoming storm. An expectant hush settled upon those whose eyes were fixed on the entrance to the Chapel. Dancing shadows began to flicker and dart through the gap. Fleeting shadows gathering speed, snarling and howling shadows. Then an echoing crash as twenty or more battle hounds hit the white doors in unison. Pandemonium ensued, crossbow bolts flew, but to no avail as the armoured beasts were terrifyingly speedy and nigh on impenetrable. Jaws snapped, as did the necks they connected with.

The guards were soon breached. Then came a blood-curdling sound, a symphony of screaming, with the metallic clatter of swords, axes and shields as an accompaniment. Fuldus' fiercest warriors were through the doors and bearing down on the scattering Brotherhood and lords alike. One such warrior, upon seeing Fuldus, dropped down onto all fours, his companion immediately using him as a step, vaulting himself into the air. In the same instant as he was airborne, he hurled a broadsword like a paper dart towards his commander.

Fuldus did not take his eyes from it and raised a mighty fist catching the sword by its hilt. As soon as he hit the floor, he began hacking at those around him. The Keeper of the

Secrets could see the tide quickly turning against his troops. Those still fighting were being butchered, the rest were already trying to escape past their attackers.

At that same moment, Fuldus saw a flash of red robes. The Keeper of the Laws had returned; then grabbing the head of his order, the two men dashed behind the curtain on the wall and vanished from sight. Fuldus carved a path towards it. One lash of his blade and the cloth was on the floor and a hitherto unseen doorway was exposed, as was a stairwell spiralling downward.

The two men ahead of him were moving surprisingly quickly. Fuldus heard a door slam and locks snapping shut. He squeezed down the stairs in pursuit and found himself on a small landing and upon reaching the door, he barged it with full force, but it held firm. The thud startled the men inside who were frantically stuffing papers into attaché cases and throwing others on the embers in the small fireplace.

The Keeper of the Secrets turned to the smaller man, and with a voice as serious as the situation they were now in, asked, "Have you dealt with them?" He grasped the other man's arm as to cause discomfort. "Did you do as we discussed? It is imperative that this proceeds as planned."

The small bald man looked earnestly at his leader. With another crash on the door, he diverted his gaze and thoughts for a second. "My lord, one is aboard, the other is in place," his voice trembled, "I secured her to the device myself." His face creased momentarily, and a solitary tear rolled on his smooth cheek. "May the gods forgive me, she was in such anguish, the noise was horrific." Before he could continue, his face stung as the older man slapped him hard.

"They are not our gods!" he shrieked. "My only concern is that she still lives!"

The smaller man composed himself and continued, "I dealt with her exactly as we said, and she is aware of the consequences if she fails us."

The door shook again, and the men returned their focus on the task at hand. They had done what they needed but still had to make good their escape. The sound of the battle was still raging. Screams of the defeated and the howls of the victorious echoed through the Chapels white halls. Fuldus heard approaching feet and prepared to defend himself but there was no attack. The footsteps belonged to Sarn and four other warriors. "Cousins," he called, "bring a battering ram." The men looked about and settled upon a marble bench. Tearing it from its fixings, they proceeded to Fuldus. He hammered his fist on the oak indicating the target, and with two shuddering blows, the door splintered.

Bounding into the chamber, to their disbelief, they found it abandoned. An up-turned chair and some empty chests but no cornered Brothers. The occupants had miraculously disappeared. Fuldus roared in frustration, he could not fathom how his quarry had escaped him. Sarn surveyed the room, logic taking over. *There must be another way out,* he thought. He skirted the perimeter of the walls, listening all the while for any sound of fleeing. Then the faintest sound of something being dropped echoed from within the fireplace.

"My lord," he called excitedly, "more stairs!"

Fuldus and Sarn sprang across its glowing embers. The fireplace opened out into a small passage. The two were hardly able to squeeze their massive frames through the narrow space. Downward they went, dark and cramped, their heads and shoulders scraping brickwork as they did, disturbing dust, cobwebs and small pieces of mortar. After a matter of minutes, they emerged in a cavern of natural rock. The floor had been quarried smooth. The walls and the ceiling were still rough with ancient stalactites hanging overhead. At the furthest end was a smooth white wall which they assumed to be a part of the Chapel's structure. Against it, they saw briefly the silhouettes of their prey vanishing through a door, which was instantly slammed shut.

The sound reverberated through the cavern. Fuldus and Sarn were there in moments, hammering fists and shoulders against the almost invisible opening. Then something happened which they had not expected. The wall itself shuddered and appeared to shift. Taken aback, the men ceased their activity. The wall moved again, making the cave echo with creaks and groans, metallic and alien. Then came the sound of hissing, squealing, and the pounding of steam engines. The wall was indeed moving.

A gap began to open up between the cave floor and what appeared to be a white ship. Sarn turned to Fuldus, "What now?" he roared over the growing noise. The distance between the vessel and the men was already sixty feet and growing by the second. The ship was becoming more visible as it receded. It resembled the Chapel, only a water-borne miniature. Instead of spires and domes, there were funnels and pistons. Two giant paddle wheels pummelled the sea creating waves, which were swamping the cave.

Fuldus picked up a rock and hurled it at the ship in frustration. It bounced from the stern and vanished into the deep. Inside the vessel, the Keeper of the Secrets had reached the bridge. Looking back towards the Chapel, he gave his first order. "Captain, destroy the cave, make sure no one can follow!" Portholes slid open and instantly, cannonballs were whistling over the heads of Fuldus and Sarn.

Realising the precarious nature of their situation, they turned and raced back to the stairwell. The white ship was sleek, speedy and rapidly escaping to the open seas. All around them was deafening destruction. Fuldus roared again as the Keeper and his ship vanished, obscured by a cloud of dust and falling rubble from the cave collapsing around them.

The two stumbled back into the stairwell, choking and half blind. They were soon back in the small room gulping down air, then quickly back to the scene of the battle, which moments before was carnage, was now at peace. Fuldus' men were piling the bodies of the dead in the centre of the great round table. Other white-uniformed guards knelt in silence, their hands on their heads. None dared to move. Hounds sniffed and snarled, hungry and impatient for any sign of resistance.

The boy who had opened the great doors and three other tribesmen had fallen during the attack. They lay separated from the rest. Their hands crossed on their chests. Covered with white linen their blood still visible and a testament to the way they died. The young warrior, Fuldus finally learned was named Clay, he had been in the Chapel since Fuldus' arrival. The only occupant of the basket loaded by the unsuspecting Brothers. His selfless actions had made their victory simple. He was taken in honour to a hilltop overlooking the sea and placed on a pyre at dawn the next day.

The Captain of the Chapel guards was thrown to the floor before Fuldus. The man was pleading for his life before Fuldus even had time to speak. "My lord," he began, "there may still be time, she could still be saved."

Fuldus dragged the man to his feet. "What are you babbling about?" he barked.

The Captain, seeing he had won a reprieve, spoke more promptly, "Hurry, my lord, follow me." He backed away a few steps, not sure of the warriors' reaction. Fuldus, however, stepped after him.

The Captain picked up his pace and was soon leading a party of a dozen hill tribesmen to the Keeper of the Secrets' private chambers. As they approached, the sound of anguished cries could be heard ahead. Sarn prodded the Captain in the back with the tip of his sword, "If this is an attempt at ambush, you know who will be the first to die."

The small quaking man turned his eyes wide, fear etched on his face. "It is her, my lord, we must hurry." He moved ahead to a door, normally locked and guarded, but now ajar. The screaming grew louder. Fuldus and his men, for the first time since their adventures had begun, were uneasy.

The door was pushed slowly open and the group filed reluctantly inside. The men could not comprehend what they were seeing, the screams were being carried on a howling wind which filled the room. There was a maelstrom of books, candles, small pieces of furniture and paintings swirling and spiralling past, clattering off one another and the walls as they went. A vortex of ash from the fireplace joined the dance.

At the centre of the maelstrom, solid and motionless stood a cruciform bedlike structure. Iron, ornate and within it, a woman fastened at the neck, her arms spread and shackled. She was howling a blood-curdling, yet pitiful scream, her eyes rolling white in her head. Her few straggly grey hairs dragged across her face by the wind. Above her, swaying menacingly were three guillotine blades, one above her throat, the other two above her wrists. It was a fearsome-looking device, the likes of which none had seen before.

"Woman!" yelled Fuldus, over the din. "Woman! Who are you?"

In the blink of an eye, all that was in motion crashed to the floor. The woman, wiry and frail, became silent and fixed Fuldus with a glare that chilled his soul.

"Speak!" Fuldus roared, not fully aware of the silence that now occupied the room. "Speak, I said!"

The woman's eyes narrowed. "Do not give me orders, little man," she hissed, trying in vain to raise her head and free her arms. She diverted her eyes to the door which slammed shut, making all within the room fearful of what might happen next. With her eyes on Fuldus again, she continued, "I have occupied these earths for an eternity, you should bow your head when you address me, Fuldus of the hills."

All eyes were now on him. "How do you know me, witch, what are you?" he demanded.

"What am I, what am I!" she screamed in response, "What I am is dying. Stabbed in the heart by that red rodent Law Keeper. Terrified, fleeing in their ship of iron, gobbling coal and wood." Her tone had changed, her anger now directed at those no longer in the room.

Fuldus sensed it and asked softly, "What is your name, my lady?"

She smiled at him. "Ah, the oaf becomes a poet," she sneered. "Do not waste your flattery on me boy, I have seen the likes of you many times before."

She beckoned him closer, he obliged by lowering his head towards her. He gagged, as he could see for the first time a blade protruding from the women's chest, seemingly coming from beneath her. She continued in a whisper barely audible, "Orphan child looking for revenge, orphan child screaming at the dark, 'Mummy, Mummy'." A low cackling laugh filled the room.

Fuldus was incensed. "Hold your tongue, hag!" he wailed. The woman mocked dismay at his outburst and in a conciliatory tone went on, "Why, my lord? I speak only the truth. I speak your truth, the truth that sustained you, fed you, made you strong."

She sucked in air through the blood clogging her throat and rasped. "I can only speak the truth; it is my curse, the curse of the Oracle."

There was a collective gasp from all those assembled. Were they really in the presence of such a legendary creature? An Oracle, a gift from the gods. A seer, a portal to divine knowledge. The Children of Summer, the peoples of the islands called them, they would only appear on the earth between May and June and at no other times. They were thought to be myth. Could she really be such a being?

Fuldus and Sarn stood their ground, the others in the party were backing towards the door. Seconds later, it was open, and they were gone.

"So, it begins to make sense," Fuldus said. "The power of prophecy, a sham," he laughed, "the infallible ability to predict."

Sarn's discomfort was taking hold and to make matters worse, the shackled woman unleashed an ear-splitting howl sending a small table dashing through the air to smash against the wall, falling in pieces to the floor. He could take no more and made a hasty exit.

"Cease your moaning, woman," said Fuldus calmly, whilst righting a chair and making himself comfortable. "I will send a healer to tend to you." The Oracle fell silent, and after a few moments returned to the subject of the Keeper of the Laws.

"You will be wasting your time my lord," she began, "the vile Brother knew his trade, but his machine failed him," she whispered, "to kill my kind, the head, hands and heart must all be taken at once."

Her wrist twisted in its restraints and her bony finger pointed to the area where the blade protruded from her chest.

Fuldus winced at the sight. "I will get a surgeon," he said, leaping to his feet.

The old woman smiled. "There is no need, my lord," she said quietly. "This one wound *will* end my life but not for a very long time."

She explained the energy within her and that which linked all peoples, places, worlds, histories past, and those still to come were the same. The injury to her heart was returning her to the source of that power. The agony she felt, though, was excruciating. Every second felt like a thousand lightning strikes. Unlike a human however, her death would be drawn out and torturous, the process sometimes taking several years, decades even.

Fuldus could not help but be moved by the old woman's plight. He dragged his chair closer to her and taking a dagger from his belt, picked the locks at her throat and wrists. He rose to his full height, apologising as he lifted and pulled her from the blade, careful not to crush her as he did. While still cradling her, with his foot he righted an overturned cot and laid her gently upon it. Free from her shackles, the room became lighter, as if the sun had begun to stream in through non-existent windows.

"Thank you, my lord," she whispered, "Fuldus, Ruler of the Islands." Fuldus could not help but smile. She continued, "Ruler today…" her voice trailed off, a smile cracked her papery lips, "…ruler of these lands forever." Fuldus went to speak, unsure of her meaning. "Listen well my lord," a cautionary tone had entered her voice, Fuldus was rapt, eager for what would come next. The woman's eyes rolled white in her head as if she were in a trance. "Rule these lands forever if you wish, my lord."

His head was spinning. "Ruler forever, how?" he wanted to know.

"It is simple," she said. "With my benefaction you can rule for an eternity; you can rule for a day. For as long as you chose." She could see Fuldus was struggling to understand. "Until you choose to end your life, you will rule, and no one, god nor man," she said with a wry chuckle, "will be able to end your life for you; you can rule forever."

Fuldus, struggling to make to make sense of what she had said, finally spoke, "I will rule these lands forever, how?" he mumbled.

"As payment for the kindness you have shown me this day, I offer the protection of my kind for as long as I live in this realm or any other," she whispered, "you will be armoured by us, infallible, deathless..." she paused to catch her breath, "...and one question also, you can ask of us one question to which only the truth will be answered."

Fuldus looked perplexed, his thoughts racing, *What question, what question should I ask?* The lady raised her hand. "Rest your mind, my lord, choose your question wisely. I shall remain on this earth until you ask it and shall pass only after its answer you have," she paused once more, "I shall leave, but our protection will remain." Fuldus and the Oracle shared a conspiratorial silence for several minutes before the lady spoke again.

"If you hunger for this," she wheezed, "consider the price?" A whimper returned to her voice. "To do this would be a monstrous thing, to do this, you must live alone, isolated, else watch all those you love age, wither and die." The words cut Fuldus to the core, albeit briefly, family was after all of the utmost importance to the hill tribes. *However,* he thought, *I have lived my life like a hermit this far, orphaned, fending for myself, hasn't it always been my destiny to be by myself?*

"You say that to rule these lands forever, I must be prepared to walk to eternity alone." A slow nod of agreement she gave. Fuldus continued, "Why would I destroy myself? When I can shape the future. I can make this world be as it should. Why? When I can have everything? Be everything. I will keep my kin at a distance, I will have no need of love, I will not fear the loss of it to the passing years when I can be as permanent as the mountains. As vast as the sky and as mysterious as the heavens. I will be king, clergy, god. I can stand alone, I will stand alone."

The Oracle chuckled. "Oh, my King," she said mockingly, "you understand nothing." Scorn hardened her voice, "You think you will be the god king?" she snorted, "The monster, it's the monster king you must become."

His face betrayed no emotion; in that instant, he knew his path. With his mouth to the Oracle's ear, he whispered, "I will keep you safe, and come to you with my question when I am ready, yet you say I must become a monster," he rose to his feet, his cold eyes fixed on the unfortunate woman below him, "Well, now is a time for monsters, so a monster I will become."

The man who entered the room was not the man who left it, no longer the young leader, wanting to right the wrongs of the past, the saviour of his people and homeland, in his place was a grim replica consumed by prophecy and the promise of never-ending power.

His transformation was as swift and brutal as that of Anglia itself. His first action on leaving the Oracle was the execution of all the members of the Brotherhood who had not fled the Chapel as well as his own troops apart from Sarn, anyone in fact he thought might have knowledge of the Oracle's existence.

The length and breadth of the country, hill tribesmen who were cheered as liberators were now reviled as they sat in occupation. The Chapel in the west was destroyed and a new capital building, The Citadel was constructed at Fulham on the banks of the river Thames. All regions now had a garrison house where the newly formed Guard of the Hill Tribes trained new conscripts. Farmers became soldiers. Arable land became foundries and munitions factories.

Steam-powered ships, a fleet of small attack frigates patrolled the coasts. Waggons with cannons mounted on them were ready to strike anywhere within the shores at a moment's notice. The mere mention of the Brotherhood of the Celestial Majesty was punishable by death. Within Fuldus' own ranks, any dissent or insubordination would be met with floggings and hard labour, usually resulting in death.

Fuldus himself with his closest aids orchestrated the changes. Laws and directives were passed unopposed. Taxes were collected to fund the new army and navy, and also Fuldus' pride and joy, a squadron of steam-powered airborne sky ships, held aloft by helium-gas balloons, sleek and terrifyingly speedy, capable of pounding a village to dust. Their roar filled the sky that first morning they saw action above the seas on the south coast near Dover. Fuldus was roused from his sleep to be told of a small flotilla of fishing boats was fleeing to Gaul, carrying upward of thirty families, men, women and children. The boats with nothing but the wind to drive them to safety were already halfway across the channel and out of range of the long guns and frigates, he was told.

Fuldus smiled, there would be no daring escape by enemies of the state this day. When the sky ships appeared hissing overhead, the flotilla surrendered immediately, but even as they lowered their sails, they were blasted to smithereens, leaving none alive. Fuldus oversaw the operation himself with the screams of families ringing in his ears.

His reputation for cruelty spread. He led his troops into action against the last of the Brotherhood's remaining infantry in the fields outside of the market town of Maidstone. His troops were outnumbered five to one, but he charged from the front regardless. Broadsword in hand, he hacked his way through the front lines to the archers at the rear. Reports say he ran through a blizzard of arrows. None of which struck him. The blows of mace and sword left no traces. The commanders of the Brotherhoods' forces fled to a nearby farm. They held a family—the farmer, his wife and five children—as their hostages, assuming them bargaining chips. Fuldus upon assessing the situation, strode to the pretty farmhouse and tore up the fence which surrounded it. He took the planks and nailed them over doors and windows. There was no negotiation, the farm and all inside were burned.

Life on the islands was now unrecognisable. Village after village, region after region, all pledged allegiance to Fuldus. But despite the totality of his control and the fear of his reprisals, rumours continued to circulate about sightings of the white ship which had escaped the day the Chapel fell, carrying the Keeper of the Secrets to safety. The ship was apparently never moored in the same place two nights in succession. When the frigates and sky ships would arrive, all they would find was gossip of what had been seen. Villages were burned, crops destroyed, but still no information was forthcoming. There was also talk of the Keeper of the Laws having been seen in Fulham, not more than two miles from the Citadel. He was said to be recruiting members, not to the Brotherhood of the Celestial Majesty, but to a new organisation. One sworn to destroy Fuldus and his new order.

For the better part of a decade, it continued, Fuldus would tighten his grip, but despite his best efforts, attacks against him were on the increase. The governors of the more isolated regions were becoming nervous. A barracks was bombed in Carlisle. Black-robed men and women would be seen before but not after such attacks. A hill-tribe sergeant was found hanged on Clapham Common and around his neck strung a sign which read *'damned to hell'*.

No matter how Fuldus stamped on those nearest geographically, the incidences still occurred. As he sat secluded in his chambers at Fulham, mulling over reports from recent years, months, and weeks. *Tomorrow*, he thought to himself, would see his authority re-established. Pomp and circumstance, a show of strength. No one would dare challenge him during the celebration of his rise to power in his own Citadel. Yet still he slept that night uneasily, cautious of what would tomorrow bring, because despite the Oracle's promises, he was beginning to feel vulnerable.

The Gift

She sat weeping for what seemed like an eternity. How had it come to this? Sitting in a windswept field, guilt-ridden and anguished. "We have to go back, this can't happen, it's not worked." The woman's face fell back to her open palms. Her hair forming a shroud around them. The two men with her turned and looked back across the city; nothing had changed. The bells of the Citadel were undisturbed. No plumes of smoke, no screams of terror, no evidence to prove their success. If they had in fact failed, they must flee.

"To your feet, Sister, it is not safe here, we must run." He grabbed her shoulder and tried to pull her to her feet as he began to retreat.

"But the girl, the..." she wept. Before she could say any more, his hand was clasped over her mouth, anger and disgust at his own part in these matters in his eyes.

"We cannot help her now, no one can," his throat began to close around the words, "She is probably dead, and Fuldus' guard is on a mission here. Now hurry, woman, away!"

The woman pulled herself to her feet. She stood and took one last look behind, "What if she is not dead and she should remember who she is?"

The older man stopped, barely able to support his own frame at the mere idea. He placed a trembling hand on her shoulder. "If that happens," he said, "pray she is not who we think she is."

The citadel was in fact far from undisturbed. The gathered crowd of dignitaries, gentle folk and commoners stood in agitated silence. Uniformed security and lesser ranks of Fuldus' bodyguard pressed them back from seeing what was happening. The golden cherubs on the vaulted ceiling of the throne room had the best vantage point. The flickering candles from the vast wooden chandeliers glinted on a guard's polished blade, at the end of it, a girl, an infant of no more than five or six years, she stood transfixed, eyes unblinking, with no semblance of fear.

"Now tell me, child, what have I done to deserve such a gift? A mannequin such as yourself. Armaments dressed in innocence," enquired Fuldus from his throne with obvious grim menace.

Nervous laughter rippled through those assembled. The child stood motionless, her arms outstretched in front of her. In her peach-soft hands was an open box of white-polished ivory with mother of pearl inlays in a fleur-de-lis motif. The box was open, its gated lid folded at its sides. Clearly visible within was a life-sized human skull, each of its teeth decorated alternately with a ruby and an emerald. More remarkable, perhaps, was the fact that it was packed with explosives connected to a rudimentary, and fortunately for those in the close vicinity, faulty triggering device.

Moments before, a battle-hound's baying had silenced the quartet of fiddlers, accompanying a slow procession of gift givers. It had become the custom on occasions such as this to bring lavish gifts for the ruler of the land.

From the four corners of the islands, rich and poor alike, came to flatter Fuldus' inflated sense of self-worth and his taste for the gaudy and excessive, which he had cultivated over the years. The hound in question had detected lignite, a volatile explosive, and once the giant wolfhound had sniffed out the source, it sprang towards the seemingly fragile child, now surrounded by Fuldus' personal bodyguard, sabres drawn, dogs straining, teeth bared, drooling, all ready to kill or die at their masters' command.

Fuldus rose to his feet. His massive frame could not hide his natural agility and grace. He danced down the three steps in front of his gilded throne to the polished, pink, marble floor. He raised his hand, candlelight glinting on the stones on his fingers. "Captain Sarn, lower your weapon, surely this angel means us no harm." The captain gratefully complied, the ornate sword was no light weight, and even with arms as muscular as his, he welcomed the rest. Fuldus leaned down towards the statue-like child, his own bulk forcing stale air from his lungs. "Child," he began with a singsong lilt, "tell me now, who sent me this beauty? Someone who knows me well. Someone who knows of my appreciation for the macabre. Someone who knows of my inexhaustible ability for mercy perhaps."

Silence was his only reply. "What is your name, child?" A momentary pause. "You don't know much of anything do you, a poor simpleton perhaps? Who has no name, no history…" a slight rasp entered his delivery, "…no return address?" The subtlety of his threats simmered just beneath the surface of his speech.

He stood upright and surveyed his audience. "I will show you all how a great man responds to such an outrageous act." He glared towards the still and emotionally detached girl. "I will deal with this child, as the law allows." This brought a muted gasp from those listening. How he revelled in such theatrics. "This child will be, from now on; my property," then puffing out his chest for the fullest effect, "I shall treat her as if she were my own daughter, and I will call her," with a smile dancing on his lips in appreciation of his own bravado, "I will call her, Little Death."

Sarn looked on in astonishment, Fuldus beckoned to him. "My beloved cousin, can you explain please, how this diminutive assassin managed to elude seven hundred uniformed men-at-arms, and one hundred and twenty of my own personal custodians?"

Sarn's bright blue eyes began to lose their shine, "My lord, I shall handle the investigation myself…"

Fuldus waved his hand in a silencing gesture. "Cousin, a captain of your stature and valiant service will do nothing of the sort, I shall deal with this mischief as it deserves to be dealt with."

A benevolent hand was outstretched to a faithful friend and came to rest on his shoulder with a firm grasp and a smile. The hand then slid slowly down his arm, meeting his wrist and removed the ivory-hilted sword from his sweating palm. The broad blade's point was lifted to meet the ornate buckle on Sarn's belt. It then began the slow deliberate slalom upwards between the pewter buttons on the black uniform. The cold flat blade raised the captain's chin. His eyes met Fuldus'.

"Thank you for your years of outstanding loyalty, my beloved friend," Fuldus had always been a man to make the most of opportunity. He pirouetted, the flash of the blade was accompanied by the unified shriek of the crowd as the last man who shared his secret of what was discovered that fateful day at the Chapel died.

Fuldus unfurled his fingers and the sword fell with a clatter that echoed in the silent hall as if to applaud his action. Then gesturing to the stunned guard behind the fallen body of Sarn, "You, what is your name?"

The tribesman quickly blinked himself back into action. "Karver, my lord."

Fuldus smiled. "How very apt. Take Little Death to the scullery." He lowered his voice, "Appoint someone to tend to her, and remember the adage, keep your friends close, but your enemies, make family."

Karver snapped a nod to his master and turned to leave. "Karver," he added, "this child may yet lead us to the conspirators and architects of this attempt on my precious life, watch her at all times." The hall was immediately cleared and Fuldus marched to his private quarters, smug in the knowledge of the Oracle's gift. A charmed life, the price was in no doubt worth it. As the chattering crowd left, the child who had been the centre of attention was ushered away to the kitchen by Karver and two of the guards. She sat motionless on a large stool used for milking goats, apparently unaware of the fuss she had caused.

Her appearance was unremarkable; she looked like any child one would encounter in many surrounding towns and cities. She had slightly tanned skin and smooth dark hair. Her features were small, her lips red. The tips of her ears projected slightly through her hair in a most appealing fashion, but it was her eyes that were the focus of her presence. Brown, they were, not hazel, but the darkest wet brown, like molasses. It was almost impossible to tell the pupil and iris apart, and still she sat motionless. Eventually a woman, one of the household staff, came hurriedly toward her. She squatted on her haunches and asked so softly, "What is your name, little angel?" and fully expecting no reply, the girl duly obliged with silence. "Little Death, is it? I think not."

At that, she rose to her feet, standing about five feet tall. The plump woman with the rosy cheeks swept the girl into her arms, and holding her close with a mothers tenderness, she whispered, "I won't be calling you Little Death," and thought for a moment, "Beth," she kissed the girl's cheek, "that will be your name." She leaned her head back to consider the girl's eyes, but still there was nothing, no sign of shock, no tears. "I will look after you now, little angel." Then hugging the girl tight, and in the softest of whispers, she said, "I am sure great things await you."

Fuldus was as usual sitting alone, his desk covered with maps of Anglia and the surrounding countries. There were piles of documents updating him as to the progress of factory building, troop numbers, the locations of arms caches, military hardware, and suchlike. The islands had begun to feel too small for his ambitious nature. His thoughts today, however, were elsewhere. He leaned forwards and picked up the ornate box that had been so dramatically presented to him. He revolved it in his hands, admiring its obvious craftsmanship.

Gaulish, from the south perhaps. The contents of the box, though, were of most interest to him. The human skull with an unmistakable smile. Teeth of rubies and emeralds. Was this the Keeper of the Secrets' skull, a genuine gift, but why the lignite? Or was it more likely a reminder from the Brotherhood of their continued presence and threat? A reminder of his own failure in letting the old man escape him. Even gazing upon it made the bile in Fuldus rise. His hatred for the Brotherhood had sustained him through many a long, lonely night, both as a boy and now a man, *but what of the girl*, he thought. *Why sacrifice the child?*

The woman had carried the now quickly renamed girl to a bedroom adjoining her own via a connecting door. The rooms were basic, but warm and clean. The beds were overly large, as was most furniture now, built that way in case it needed to accommodate the bulk of one of the hill tribesmen. The girl was bathed in warm, soapy water and put in a clean night gown. She was offered some milk and cheese, both which you could not say she refused, she just seemed not to notice them. Her guardian stoked the fire and within minutes, Beth was soundly asleep.

The woman who was charged with Little Death's care had worked at the citadel since it was finished. She had attended Fuldus' on his official birthday celebrations on a few occasions. The first time she spilled some red wine on the marble floor, which he had made her lick up with her tongue in front of the other staff and assembled attendants. She still remembered the indignity and the fury she felt that day and like many, longed for a chance to teach him some manners.

The citadel had been her home since she and those like her had found themselves displaced and dispossessed after the invasion. She had started to work as kitchen assistant, chambermaid and cleaner, it was that or starvation. In the early days, payment was a scrap of food, if you were lucky. She would fight the dogs and other staff for a dry place she could lay her head when she was finally allowed to rest.

Her name was Emma. Her father was hanged by the Scandinavians and her mother shot down trying to escape the beaches two days before the Hill Tribes had driven the Scandinavians back to the sea. Her life had been arduous for the subsequent years. Now though she had been given a task, one that she could relish, a chance to protect someone and show them life did not have to be a struggle, that it could have purpose, and wonderful possibilities.

For the first two months of her time in Fulham, Little Death saw nothing of the citadel. Its passages and towers remained a mystery to her. The two rooms, the one where she slept and the other were Emma slept, plus the kitchens were all she knew of where she now lived. She had seen nothing of the big man who towered over her in her dreams, but lots of the man Emma called Karver; he was like a shadow. She only ever went outside to collect eggs from the cobbled courtyard. She would laugh at the rusty brown hens as they erupted squawking from their coops each morning as her treasure hunt began. Other than this momentary expression of childlike normality, she had made no other sound since her arrival on that first day.

Emma, seven times a week, at one o'clock, would attend Fuldus' office to update him on any developments. Each day she would feel the same uneasy knot form in her stomach as she approached his chambers. She was once kept waiting there for the entire day and most of the night before the bodyguards ushered her into the room. Emma knew Little Death; Beth was safe with the head cook, Mrs Cooper, but she did not appreciate having to leave her charge for so long a time. When she did finally stand before him on that day, he said, "I suppose you have nothing new to tell me," but before she could answer, she felt the sting of his knuckles across her jaw which sent her sprawling to the floor. She crawled out of the room with his curses still ringing in her ears.

This is how life continued. The egg-hunts each morning and the child's silence. Summer turned to the gold of the autumn, before old man winter swept away her finery. The Yule celebrations, as much as they were, came and went. The long cold trek to spring was lightened though for Emma, still happy in her work, watching Beth grow stronger daily. No longer the waif who had arrived so spectacularly nearly a year before.

As much as the other domestic staff would not believe it, Emma swore she was almost certain that their lord and master would watch Beth from his window on her morning egg hunt. "I saw him," she said earnestly, "Happy he was." At that, Mrs Cooper roared with laughter, the only reason she believed that would make him happy was because he had Beth in his musket sight.

The child continued to grow and was quite tall for her age. There were other children at the citadel to compare her with, although they were rarely seen. A year earlier, a young boy had been killed by a battle-hound after climbing into the kennels, and Fuldus, upon hearing the news, sent a veterinary doctor to check if the dogs were okay, after all he said, "They usually only eat mutton."

Emma had become so used to Karver's presence that she hardly noticed him anymore. One long rainy day, when Beth seemed very out of sorts and chose to stare into the flickering fires of the kitchen, Emma enquired of Karver, his first name.

He could not help but smile. "Gram," he replied, "Gramlius Karver, son of Darius."

Emma sensed his pride, "Well, Gram, as we spend so much time together, tell me about yourself."

Karver trotted through his early life in the hills. Uneventful it was, *Apart from avoiding raiding parties*, he laughed. Then, one day he was introduced to his cousin and soon to be leader of the Hill Tribes. The Brotherhood had sent many hunting parties to his village, he and his family would escape into the mountains, only to return and find their huts burned and livestock rustled. Fuldus vowed this would not go unpunished. Karver described the organising of the tribes into one army and again Emma could hear the admiration in his voice.

The Brotherhood had always been Fuldus' true target. However, when the Scandinavians arrived, they gave his plans another layer of legitimacy. He had impressed his cousin in battle and was soon a member of the elite Guard. Gram Karver was sworn to protect Fuldus and it was a task he would not shrink from, he swore to Emma.

"I would gladly die for the man," he exclaimed. "I will protect him from all threats, he saved me and my people from extinction." Despite his obvious, and as he saw it, justified pride. *His voice was too loud,* Emma thought, *for the kitchen.*

Then on that fateful day of Little Death's arrival, he found himself promoted again. He eyed the child distrustfully, she had, after all, arrived armed to the teeth. Emma momentarily felt fearful for her sweet Beth. Then his mood mellowed. "But you, Emma, what of you?" he questioned.

Emma explained that like most people after the invasion, she had been put to work and those sad events had left her no family at all.

Karver raised his hand and pointed, "The chain you wear, was it your mother's?" he asked softly.

Emma's fingers fumbled with the fine gold chain at her neck, then hurriedly, she pulled her collar loose, so it disappeared from view. She raised her head and smiled, "That is all that remains of my old life." Her eyes moistened, and at that, she reached out and gave Karver's rough hand a gentle squeeze. He was so taken aback by the softness of her touch, all his questions immediately ceased.

Emma continued her daily updates, but no sooner had she said the girl remained mute, Fuldus would fly into a rage. She would have to bolt from his sight, dodging blows or flying desk ornaments and the like. Beth had been at Fulham three full years; the time was easily counted with the passing of Fuldus' lavish annual celebrations. Emma treated it as Beth's birthday also.

The sunlight was already streaming in her bedroom when she rose the morning of what she calculated to be Beth's eighth or ninth birthday. Emma washed quickly and put on a fresh smock, then pinning back her hair, she picked up a small bunch of wildflowers she had collected the previous day. Then tapping gently on the connecting door to Beth's room, opened it slowly so not to startle the girl, she entered and whispered, "Happy birthday, my little angel."

She drew back the curtains, so the sunlight would fall on the girl's bed, warming and waking her. She turned with the posy held out in front of her to surprise the child, when she would reluctantly open her eyes. The early morning glow of the sun illuminated the bed as planned, but panic struck her. She let out a sharp cry, the flowers fell to the plain wooden floor. The bed was empty, Beth was nowhere to be seen.

She quickly checked under the blankets, the corners of the room, her room, under her bed, the small cupboard where she kept her own few scant belongings. The window was still bolted shut, just as it was the night before, so no exit had it become.

Pulling the main door to the rooms open, she screamed at the top of her voice, "Beth!"

No response. Karver awakened at the cry and fell from the stool where he had been sitting. Springing to his feet, he instantly drew his sword. "What in the name of Hades, woman?" he cursed.

"Beth, Little Death, the girl, she's gone." Emma was frantic and pacing. Karver dashed into the room, the sound of furniture being tossed around echoed along the hallway from inside.

He emerged just as panicked as the servant woman who was now running along the hall calling hysterically. Karver was quickly up with her, he clasped his hand over her mouth. "Do you know what he will do to you if he finds out you let the child escape?" he growled threateningly in her ear. She relaxed and breathed deeply through her nose, and he released her.

She spun quickly and faced him. "I would imagine he will do to me the same he does to you when you tell him you were asleep on guard duty!" she bellowed. She continued her search with the fearful man in close pursuit.

The search continued, taking in the hen houses, kitchens and pantries. Where could she be, she knew no other part of the citadel, where had she gone? The most awful possibility swept through Emma's thoughts: *the kennels*.

"Oh, my gods, the kennels!" she screamed.

Karver bounded past the now sobbing Emma, pulling open the wrought iron gate that separated the courtyard from Fuldus' guards' quarters and the kennels. He turned to the woman, saying, "Stay here, if she is in the kennels, you will not want to see it."

The next three minutes passed like an eternity. No clues could be heard from the other side of the gate. She was quietly wailing to herself, the most horrific visions forcing their way into her mind's eye. Finally, after what seemed like an age, the gate swung open again. Karver stood there, pale but empty handed. "Nothing, nothing," he panted, "which in one way is a good thing. Think, woman, where else might she have gone?"

Emma could genuinely think of no other place the child knew. "What if she has been taken?" she sobbed.

"Let's hope for both our sakes that's not what has happened," said Karver, looking towards Fuldus' window. They both knew the consequences should that be the case.

A small face from the windows above the courtyard watched as Emma and the man named Karver continued to dash about. *Egg hunt,* thought Beth, as she looked on impassively then turning away to continue with her exploration. She had found herself in a long passage with wall-mounted sconces. Candle stubs, all that remained after a long night's work. She had woken for no reason, with no idea of the time and wandered past the sleeping adults, unaware of the pandemonium this would cause.

The floor beneath her light steps creaked and groaned, and apart from her breathing, this was the only sound to be heard. Her feet appeared to have a mind of their own, wandering wherever they wanted to, walking with a purpose known only to themselves. She found herself outside a door, beside which were two sleeping guards, the same as Karver, just much smaller. Her tiny footsteps did not make enough sound to wake them. Neither did the door opening and closing. The room she entered was dark and warm. Thick drapes on the window shrouded everything in shadow. All that was visible were shapes that resembled the mountains in the west, and more darkness.

Embers from the fireplace painted the floor orange, and when stepped upon, it was warm and comforting. Her fingers drifted past the hanging coal shovel and poker, making them chime softly like distant bells. Another door bled light to the floorboards, paler like the light in the corridor outside. A candle could be seen through the crack in the door sitting on a bedside table. The bed moved up and down with laboured breathing and snores. Curiosity made her enter the room and examine the occupant of the bed more closely. The face was thinner than she remembered, but it was most certainly the big man she saw in her dreams. She remembered him well, she only ever had two dreams she could recall. The big man was in one, and the beautiful garden in the other.

She stood gazing at him as he began to stir, a tiny hand reached out and brushed his cheek. The bulk under the piles of fur and silk flicked a giant finger, as if to shoo a fly. The soft hand did the same and got the same response. A chuckle rose from Beth's throat as if she had just invented a new game. It continued for a dozen more rounds, before the flicking became more animated and accompanied by grunts, this only made her chuckle more. Finally, the grunting became a growl, and the growl, sleepy words, "Who, who is there?" The man sat bolt upright and raised the candle. He scanned the room but saw no one. Unseen Beth had slid under the bed, silently giggling as she went.

"Who's there?" roared the now wide-awake man. He continued to look left and right, certain he was not alone. Reaching slowly under the heap of pillows, he produced a horn-handled dagger. He knelt up on the bed, his eyes now focused, but he could still see no one. The shouts from inside the room had roused the guards outside and one came dashing into the room, carrying a lighted torch.

"My lord, did you call?" asked the sentry cautiously. Fuldus was now out of his bed. Beth could see his huge bare bony feet not more than a yard from where she hid, smiling. The feet walked towards the door and returned with more light upon them.

Fuldus had taken the torch and told the guard to watch the doorway. He was not sure what was happening, but he was always ready to repel an attack. The sound of a sword being unsheathed rasped unseen into the air.

"This is your last chance to show yourself," said Fuldus with a calm authority. The girl was now unsure if this was a game after all. She shifted nervously and scratched the floor; in doing so, both the men instantly snapped their stare to where the sound emanated. Fuldus, with one leap, was back on his bed with his sword ready to plunge through the mattress and whoever lay beneath it. He raised his hands, stretching his arms to their fullest above his head, "This is your last chance," he snarled, "show yourself." He was just about to thrust the enormous sword downwards, when the bedroom door burst open with such ferocity, that it was nearly lifted from its hinges.

"Wait, my lord!" screamed Emma. She knew what very real danger she was in now, but undaunted, she dived to the floor and slid under the bed. There was a momentary pause and then she emerged, pulling the now visibly shaken girl by the wrists.

Fuldus glared at Emma. "What is the meaning of this?" he demanded, "Why is she here?"

Karver had now sidled into the room and was standing, hoping not to be noticed. Emma's mind raced. How exactly was she going to explain the child's disappearance and then her bursting into her master's private quarters whist screaming like a mad woman? Emma cleared her throat, but then something that none of them expected happened.

"I wanted to tell you that I have rediscovered my voice," said Little Death calmly. "But in my excitement, I ran from my bed and did not inform either my nurse or my guardian."

All eyes looked on in astonishment at her. She spoke with such confidence and eloquence it was hard to believe she had not been heard from before.

She continued, "Please, do not be angry with my Emma or Mr Karver. If anyone is to be punished, it should be me."

For as long as he could remember, no one had addressed Fuldus with such candour, and he was trying not to explode with either rage or laughter. He was also aware of how ridiculous he must have looked, standing on his bed with his broadsword held aloft while still wearing his nightgown. Emma's eyes were welling with tears, her Beth had spoken, but not only spoken, she had spoken in her defence. Karver had taken the opportunity to drop to one knee, as was his usual position when he was in the presence of his lord, hoping against hope that Fuldus would believe the girl's story.

Fuldus stepped to the floor and allowed his sword to drop to the soft comfort of his bedclothes. He raised his hand and gestured to the door. "Everyone out!" he ordered. The party began to back out of the room, "Not you, Little Death, you remain." The door was quickly closed, and the pair were alone. "So," he began, "you have rediscovered your voice. Where, may I ask, has it been hiding all this time?" There was almost a jovial tone in his delivery. He glanced back towards where she was concealed moments before. "No surprises for me this time, I trust."

Beth looked at him, confused by his last statement. "Surprises, what do you mean?"

He could hear genuine puzzlement in her voice. "What?" he asked, "Do you remember of how you arrived here, and where you were before?"

The girl walked to the massive bed and clambered up on the mattress; it was indeed as comfortable as it looked. "Well," she began, "I woke one morning, and Emma asked me to help her collect eggs." Her eyebrows moved closer together, as if she were struggling to recall the exact details. Then she looked at Fuldus with her trusting brown eyes and said, "Before that, I, I…remember…"

Fuldus waited with bated breath. Was he finally going to find out who had sent her? "Yes, child," he softly urged.

Beth's head was beginning to swim, and nausea was taking hold, "I remember you." No sooner had the words left her lips, she fell from the bed and lay unconscious on the cold floorboards.

Fuldus darted towards her scooping her up as he did. He took only a few paces and he was at the window, which he quickly opened. The sun was just beginning to rise above the citadel walls and the sky outside was already a delicate shade of blue. The cool morning air had had the desired effect and the girl began to stir. Her eyelids flickered, a soft smile formed on her lips and she relaxed in the giant's arms, then turning her head towards him and with her eyes still closed, she whispered, "Please don't send me away."

Fuldus the monster, the ruler of all he surveyed, swallowed hard to control himself, and spoke softly so no one else would hear, "No, child, you are going nowhere; you are home."

The events of the rest of the day went at a hectic pace. Emma was called before Fuldus and chastised for her lack of control. Karver was flogged in the cobbled yard. The two guards who were quite obviously asleep when Little Death had entered Fuldus' chambers, were not so fortunate. They were thrown to the battle hounds.

Emma was told to gather her things and move to a room nearer to Fuldus', she would be next to Little Death's new accommodation. The three rooms were connected to one another just like Emma and Beth's had been before. Emma was told to appoint a tutor to see to Little Death's education. She had obviously been tutored by somebody and Fuldus saw this as the best way to jog the girl's memory and possibly gain access to her previous life. Emma was still reeling from the day's events and was itching to talk some more with Beth.

However, since her dramatic speech, she had been with the dressmaker. Fuldus' child was to accompany him to the celebrations where she would be presented to the peoples of the islands. It was just then the connecting door to Emma's quarters opened and Beth entered. She rushed to her nurse and they embraced for minutes. The dressmaker had followed her into the room with two dresses: one for Beth and the other, unbelievably was for Emma. She had been told she was, from this day forwards, never to leave the girl's side. Her punishment would not be wished away by the charms of Fuldus' charge next time. They were to dress and be in the anti-chamber behind the throne room at noon, Fuldus and his entourage would join them then.

Fuldus sat alone in his office, he had been in the citadel too long and yearned to return to his homelands; he wanted to see the mountains of his childhood. He had decided that he would tour the isles and he would take Little Death with him. *Those who had sent her,* he thought, *might try and retrieve her.* Flushing them from their cover. He would travel west, the home of the Brotherhood, perhaps the trip might trigger something in his child's memory.

The lavish celebrations went without incident. Gifts and feasting. The one subject on everyone's mind, however, was the appearance of the would-be girl assassin, now seated at the right hand of the man she was sent to kill. Little Death did not know what to make of all the fuss. As soon as news spread through the crowd, gifts were being brought for her also. China-faced dolls, delicate necklaces, earrings, silks and satin were spread before her, while Fuldus looked on satisfied that the news of her reappearance would spread to the four corners of the islands.

The Boy

School had finished for the day. School was a tent in the middle of a city of other tents and small huts. Shia was a young boy with an eager mind, his teacher Mister Koba had told him so. Shia, when in school, liked to read, write and draw pictures. But when the evening sun was at its coolest, he liked to go fishing and explore the surrounding dunes and dry grassy hills.

After a fruitless trip to one of his favoured fishing spots, Shia returned to his hut. He ate a small meal with his sister. When she had finished eating, he made sure she cleaned her plate and her face and put her to bed before reading her a story. It was a favourite of hers about a goat herd who killed a giant beast and became a hero. Once she was sound asleep, he sat quietly to do his homework.

Mister Koba had given each member of his class a book, in which he wanted them to write each day about themselves. He said it was important for people to understand one another, and the best way for that to happen was for people to learn about each other's lives. *So be honest,* he thought.

Shia thought Mister Koba was both the wisest man and kindest man he had ever met. He enjoyed his lessons and always looked forward to going to school. He sat and thought for a few minutes and finally picked up his pencil and opened his notebook. He liked the way it would try and close itself when he let go of it because it was so new, and how the pages were smooth, but the cover felt like dry palm leaves.

When Shia would concentrate, his tongue would stick from the corner of his mouth and his friends would laugh and copy him. He didn't mind, though, he liked making people laugh, he smiled briefly to himself before remembering what he had been told. Mister Koba had said people should be honest, and so he began to write,

"My name is Shia. I am eleven years old. I have been in this camp now for I think eight months. My village was burned by men who said we worshipped a false god. They said the men of our village were preaching hatred and trying to kill the men and the families in the next village who said their prayers to another god. My mother pleaded with them, saying we were peaceful, and we didn't know any bad men. They did not listen to her and they killed her in front of me and my little sister.

The kind people took us in and all the other people from the villages and towns near us; we all live together in this camp now. We have very little food and a lot of us are sick. We must keep moving around because we are hated for what we believe in. The way we look, the way we dress, and the way we speak. They say, 'You are not like us,' and chase us away.

I look at them, and all I see are families who eat dinner and children who play games. They say prayers and sing songs. That is all we do. I want to stop running now. I want to sleep soundly and not hear my sister cry at night. I want this to stop."

The boy looked around. He had become accustomed to talking to himself about things, but this time it felt like someone was listening. He could hear breathing, and not just his own. Tears rolled into the corners of his now smiling mouth. He pulled himself to his feet and stepped outside into the cool damp evening.

Suddenly screams were filling the air, the huts on the far edge of the camp were ablaze, their straw roofs crackling, the smoke releasing glowing embers into the sky. Club wielding, white-robed men were running towards him. He looked to the pale full moon, then falling to his knees he forced his hands into the earth.

The Message

The day dawned bright and balmy like the one before it. The weather was perfect for the workers in the marketplace, which was immediately outside the citadel entrance. The square opened out wide in front of the large reinforced gates that protected Fuldus' palace. Around the perimeter was a ramshackle assortment of shanty dwellings, home to the variety of labourers who populated the market six days a week. Wednesday was the only day there was no trade, as the square became a drill and parade ground for the citadel's troops. Mock battle scenarios were acted out like the weekly dramas popular at the playhouse on the other side of the river Thames, to which the citadel was connected by a stout stone bridge. Along the bridge, at its centre was a row of three-storey buildings. At the ground level were shops: there was butchery, baker, smithy, wheelwright and a brewery that doubled as a sugar and spice merchant. Above the stores were the owners and their families living quarters.

The bridge had a strictly enforced traffic system. Carts pulled by oxen could only enter after sundown on the proviso they should be gone before the following dawn. The citadel guards took no excuses for loitering. Goods, waggons, livestock and even their owners were known to be tossed over the side of the bridge in the past, so none outstayed their welcome. Pedestrians could come and go as they pleased, but only members of the market trade guild enjoyed the real freedom of the market. They were permitted to erect shelters for staff and storage, but they paid dearly for the rights and privileges of membership. A hefty bond was deposited with the citadel treasurer; this bought protection, immunity from harassment and above all, the freedom to trade. Guild members also swore an allegiance to Fuldus and acted as his eyes and ears. Gossip was a commodity in plentiful supply these days amongst the inhabitants of the city. The slightest suspicion of any treasonous talk was to be brought to the attention of Fuldus' military intelligence with much sensational detail and of course, names and addresses.

The officers of the department had become known as the Night Terrors, as unsuspecting citizens laid their heads to sleep, doors would be smashed in and the black uniformed 'Disappearance Operatives' would make arrests on the strength of whispers and finger pointing. All you needed to do to make sure some poor soul would receive a visit was to tip off a guard about those with sympathies for the Brotherhood, and the people in question would vanish like smoke in a high wind. Some said guild members used the department to remove business competitors, or suspicious husbands, a handsome rival. What was certain, of those who received a visit, very few returned to finish their night's sleep.

That morning there was plenty of new gossip to trade. Those who had been up and about, setting out stalls and filling them with fruit and vegetables and the likes, had seen columns of guards filing in and out of the citadel all night long. Carriages were being readied. Rumour had it the great man himself would be seen for the first time in months. Those who had attended or knew someone who had attended the celebrations on the day previous could speak of nothing other than the mysterious child.

"Dressed in gold, she was," they said, "at his right hand the whole time."

"Troops are preparing for a grand tour," they were saying, and all corners of the islands would be visited. The child was to accompany him first west, then north to his homeland. Every detail seemingly known to all and sundry. The soft murmurs in the square slowly climbing in volume with the rising sun.

Bleary-eyed business owners would soon emerge from their bridge houses and check none of their employees were still holed up in their hovels in the square. None dared, and once more the market was ready to serve the citizens of Fulham.

One trader, a permanent fixture of the market, was a local character known as Ned the Knife. He had several aliases, Silus Sharpener and the Axe Grinder among them. Ned pushed a red and green barrow onto the bridge every morning accompanied by the jingle of three bells that sat atop his mobile workbench. The cart looked something like a three-wheeled penny-farthing. It had handles and a seat at the back. Ned would sit when he was working, peddling furiously to make the grinding wheel in the centre of the cart whizz and hum. Ned was the man to see when your knives and the like were blunt.

He had ridden his barrow for nigh on forty years, and the paintwork, once bright and vivid, was now showing its age, as was Ned himself. He was a tall thin man with the air of a gentleman who had fallen on hard times. His sturdy boots always shone though. The moleskin breeches with buttons at the ankle had seen better days, as had his leg of mutton sleeved shirt and his ratty excuse for a neckerchief. His voluminous shirt and protruding ribs were neatly contained within a herringbone waistcoat which was as red as his wagon used to be.

Years of sharpening had taken their toll; he was blind now in his left eye, damage, it was said, from a stone chip spinning from his grinding wheel, or a knife fight in a city tavern, depending on who you spoke to first. Above his blind eye was the most spectacular eyebrow you could imagine, unkempt and feral. His right eye was groomed, sporting a monocle, for extra accuracy when he worked. His skin, having worked outside all his life, was as weathered as his cart, he had a complexion like baked leather. Its brown hue offset by a grizzled grey and auburn handlebar moustache. His head, long since bald, was protected by a forlorn-looking bowler hat.

Most in the market gave him a wide berth, he had a fearsome and richly deserved reputation for having a short and violent temper. He would pass through the market crowds unimpeded.

"Dull and blunt," he would mutter as he trundled past his fellow market workers, as an insult or a reference to his trade, no one was sure. Making conversation did not come easy to him. His customers would pass him a blunt blade and he would pass it back ready to go about its business. That was the way he liked it, and nobody saw a reason to try and change the way he worked.

This particular morning, he set his cart at the end of the market closest to the citadel gates. He seated himself and set sparks flying while sharpening his personal collection of blades, which were secreted all over his body. In belt loops, hidden pockets in his waistcoat and trousers. His hatband held at least a dozen. His favourites were the bone-handled throwing knives and a fine stiletto he kept in his sleeve. He worked like a man possessed, sharpening then testing the keenness of each blade on a block of wood which had a thousand slashes cut into it. With that task complete he sat back and raised his head to look to the highest window in the citadel wall, perhaps to ponder the goings on inside, or merely to avoid the gaze of those around him.

One of the first out and about in the market that morning was Mrs Cooper of the citadel kitchen, she had made her usual visits looking only for the best of produce not catered for within the mighty walls where she lived and worked. Honey and cinnamon were top of her list along with vanilla pods and wild strawberries. A small weasel of a man called Saxon, a guild member and all-round nasty piece of work according to just about everyone, including his wife, was her first port of call. He was the only trader permitted to sell spices, so their quality was not always what should be expected, but his honey was second to none. They exchanged pleasantries, the weather, how was Mrs Saxon and the children. In fact, Mrs Copper did not care how Mrs Saxon was, as two years previously they had come to blows whilst in a dispute over scotch Bonnet chillies. The result was, Mrs Saxon, a much smaller woman than Mrs Cooper, was doused with buttermilk and chased from the market, shamefaced and stinking like a clumsy milkmaid. No one laughed openly for fear of Mr Saxon's friends in high places. The only thing that kept Mrs Cooper safe was Fuldus' love of her wild strawberry tarts. After passing brief moments with a few other acquaintances, she found herself at the stall of one Mother Dove-Coop, so named because she had reared white doves for the past ninety years. She was almost as blind as a mole; her hearing, however, was said to have been stolen from a bat. She was also the shrewdest of businesswomen. She knew all the secret places where only the finest and sweetest wild woodland strawberries grew, and Mother Dove-Coop charged a pretty penny for them in return.

Mrs Cooper positioned herself amongst the baskets of fruits, which sat under the red and white-striped cloth awning of Mother Dove-Coop's market stall. "Good morning, Mother!" she called, making the old woman turn as sharply as her brittle old bones would allow her.

"Gods in heaven, woman, how many times have I told you?" she snapped. "It's my eyes that are as dull as your wits," she sucked in a quick breath, "but my ears and my tongue, on the other hand, are as sharp as ever."

There was a pause, and then both women gave a knowing laugh. "How are you, Agnes?" asked the older woman. She was one of a select few who knew Mrs Cooper's first name, and one of an even more select few who felt comfortable using it.

"I am very well, Mother, very well indeed." she chuckled. "I had to give that reprobate Axe Grinder a wide berth, I practically fell over him as I came out the door this morning," she said. Surveying the display in front of her she selected the largest punnet of strawberries on offer. A price was quickly settled upon and the goods carefully wrapped.

"Agnes," enquired Mother Dove-Coop sweetly, "will you take a cup of nettle and honey tea, dear?"

Mrs Cooper declined. She was already turning to leave. "Sadly not," she began, "I have some tarts to bake and wrap for a journey, our lord and master is on the move." She glanced furtively about, and leaned towards her old friend, "Off to Lizard Island, he is, and the little princess is going with him." She tapped the side of her nose with her index finger and dashed off in the direction of the kitchens.

When the sound of Mrs Cooper's clogs had receded into the growing market din, Mother Dove-Coop sat herself on a stool behind the fruit display. Her eyes narrowed, "Bloody, Axe Grinder," she tutted. She saved her real disdain, though, and repeated, "Our lord and master, lord indeed," she coughed and spat on the ground nearby in disgust. She twisted to her left and picked up a thin slither of paper from a small clay pot. From inside her apron, she produced a stick of hardened charcoal that had been sharpened to a fine point for writing. She began scratching on the paper and after a few words were laid down, reached beneath her display of fruits to a large square wicker bin. She deftly slid her hand under the hinged lid, causing an unseen commotion of feathers and cooing. She sat back upright and within her grasp was a dove as white as a magnolia flower.

Her fingers, surprisingly nimble, scrolled the paper around the leg of the bird. She then fastened it in place with an ornate brass ring which was hinged on one side; it snapped shut with a silent click. Then standing again, she lifted the lid on the wicker basket with her foot, and as the sky filled with birds, she released the messenger bird with them. The pale blue morning sky was suddenly alive. The sun's rays illuminating the cloud of doves, as a sea of faces looked up. A moment of beauty to soak in, before returning to their daily business. The birds, unaware of their effect, circled the market in unison before flying out across the river.

After a short flight, one of the doves landed softly on a windowsill, its gentle call permeating the room above the bustling city street. A small bony hand scooped up the bird. "Hello, what have you there?" the occupant of the room asked. The bird was firmly but gently grasped, and the massage removed, eager fingers unfurled the tiny scroll. Lips moving but no sound, the note read: *"They are on the move. Prepare the Sisters of Vengeance."* A gasp of anticipation and delight filled the lungs of the reader, and a thin smile spread across the red lips of the Keeper of the Laws.

The birds were seen from a tower too, a childish face full of glee and mischief watched from a window high above the citadel courtyard. Far below the highest watchtower, Beth could see waggons being readied. Fuldus' personal guard preparing carthorses and battle hounds. Two squads of twelve men, heavily armoured, had been handpicked to protect the first leg of the journey west. More troops would be added as they reached the long road, a full three-day ride, she had been told by Emma, that stretched all the way to the ancient megalithic stone circles that marked the beginning of the territory considered to be the stronghold of the outlawed Brotherhood.

From below, Beth could hear her name being called. She ignored it.

"Beth!" it came again, closer this time. "Beth!" This time not more than a little agitated. "Beth, for the love of…" The door to the tower swung open. "Sometimes," continued the voice, "I think you just like to see me suffer."

Beth turned to Emma, who was scarlet in the face from her climb of what Beth knew to be at least two hundred stone steps. "Sorry, Emma," she began, "did you say something?" Beth could not keep the smile from her face. Emma pinched her eyebrows together in an attempt to look menacing; this only caused Beth to laugh aloud. "Don't make that face Emma, please, it is most unattractive." She started towards the door, continuing as she went, "It makes you look boss-eyed and ever so slightly like the village idiot."

With that, she bolted through the doorway and began to hurtle headlong down the steps of the tower, her bare feet on the cold smooth stone and her hand outstretched racing over the rough walls. Behind her, she could hear the mock outrage of Emma trying to keep up. "You cheeky. Well, I never, you just wait, madam," panting punctuated every other word, "I'll give you village idiot."

Beth cleared the bottom of the stairs at a pace and not having time to stop, she careered into the oncoming guards and kitchen staff in the courtyard loading the waggons for the journey.

"Ah, there you are," chuckled Mrs Cooper, "and if you're here, then the Lady Emma can't be far away." Mrs Cooper was correct. No sooner had the words drifted to silence, Emma came bounding from the stairwell, red and panting. "Honestly, look at the both of you, like two street urchins. Put some shoes on young lady," the cook scolded mockingly, "My Lord Fuldus is searching for the pair of you, quite breezy, he is too," a pause punctuated her delivery, "by his standards, that is."

But as often was the way in the citadel, the mood of all could quickly change. A roar reverberated throughout the square. "Karver!"

The volume and the ferocity of the call made everyone within earshot jump with something approaching terror. Fuldus appeared to the left of the cobbles, bouncing the door against the wall as he crashed through it. Four pike-wielding foot soldiers closely followed him. Karver, still sore from the flogging he had recently received, put down the barrel he was carrying towards the pantry waggon and turned sheepishly towards the onrushing mountain of fury that was heading his way.

Before Karver had time to enquire what was happening, he was grasped by the throat and dangling in mid-air at the end of Fuldus' mighty grip. "Explain yourself," hissed his master, "explain, explain."

Karver was in no position to explain anything, he was finding it difficult to breathe. Next, he was flying through the air, a solid waggon wheel stopping and simultaneously winding him. He was alert enough to kneel before Fuldus, but not looking up, he coughed, "Explain what, my lord?"

Fuldus thumbed a gesture at the guards. Two of them walked to the cowering man and pulled him upright. Fuldus leaned in, "Explain this," he growled, and with that, he slowly opened his hand.

As he did, a small, round, golden medallion began to slide from his fingers along the length of a fine golden chain. The medallion halted its gravity-driven decent and swayed back and forth. A unified gasp rose from those assembled. The medallion quite clearly bore the emblem of the Brotherhood.

The rising sun, an image not seen in public since the destruction of the Chapel, in the hand of the man who had seen it done. Those around him mirrored the look of horror on Karver's face. "My lord, I ain't never, it ain't mine, it…"

Fuldus cut him off in mid flow. "It was found in your quarters! Hidden under a floorboard! With books and other such charms and nonsense." Fuldus once more had Karver by the throat, this time with both hands. "You will be praying for the return of your Brothers no more. You who have called me cousin, you treacherous viper!" Karver's eyes rolled in his head. A cracking, soft and gentle like eggshells under foot, made Fuldus' vice-like grip loosen. Karver's body went limp. Fuldus opened his hands and watched him fall lifeless to the floor.

Emma pulled Beth to her, spinning the child around so she could look no more. Her hand clasped at the back of her head to keep her in place. Fuldus inhaled deeply through his nostrils. He could feel his composure returning. He looked at the golden emblem still entwined between his fingers and raised it above his head. "Does anyone else wish to pledge allegiance to the Brotherhood?" he growled whilst surveying the silent courtyard.

He hurled the emblem to the floor and spat a curse at Karver's dead body. "Take him," he barked to the shaken guards, "hang him in the marketplace, let the crows and gulls have him, he will be a warning to any who share his desire to return to the dark ages." He glared at the motionless crowd. "This is what piety gets you," he screamed, pointing at the body on the cobbles.

The crowd began to separate as what had been Karver was dragged towards the citadel gates and its final resting place.

The fury which had engulfed Fuldus was now gone. He clapped his hands, and in unison, the staff and guards alike returned to their duties. He spun on his heel, his eyes meeting Emma's. She could barely hide her revulsion at what she and

Beth had just witnessed. Fuldus was not completely impervious to it. An awkward smile returned to his face, "Ah, there is my little angel," he hummed. "Are you ready for our adventure?"

Emma released Beth's head from her grasp, and the child turned to face the man who, moments before, was a seething mass of murderous rage and greeted him with a sweet smile and a cheery, "Yes, Emma and I are packed and ready to leave whenever you give the word." Anyone within earshot was stunned; it was as if the child had witnessed nothing more than a petty playground squabble. She seemed immune to the fury and the endless horrors that accompanied Fuldus on a daily basis.

He squatted down before her. "Then take yourself to the white waggon and make yourself comfortable," he suggested gently.

Rising again, he looked towards Emma, "See she has everything she needs and take your place in the waggon behind." With that, Fuldus turned to walk away.

"My lord," came the slightly quaking voice of the nurse. "My lord."

Fuldus stopped and turned, irritation once more returning to his eyes. His top lip curled. "What is it?" he said, his teeth barely parting as he did.

"My lord, Little Death had become quite comfortable with," she gestured hesitantly towards the gates, "that particular guard."

Fuldus was now more interested than he had at first been. "Your point?" he enquired.

"Little Death is now without a personal bodyguard," she informed him. Fuldus assured her he would appoint one immediately and again turned to leave.

"My lord," began Emma again, "may I suggest?" Fuldus could not believe his ears and found himself once more turning back, with increasing irritation towards Little Death's nurse. Emma wasted no time, "I know of a guard she is also comfortable with, my lord. He usually tends the battle hounds." Fuldus continued to listen so Emma continued to talk. "His name, I believe, is Thompson."

The waggons were all but ready to leave when an official from Fuldus' staff entered the kennels. The six or so men working stopped what they were doing immediately and stood to attention.

"Which one of you is Thompson?" asked the uniformed man in a surprisingly polite and genial manner. The few seconds of silence which followed were shattered by the sound of a metal shovel falling to the ground with a sharp clang!

The man whose grasp had just failed him stepped forwards, "That would be me, sir, Jasper Thompson." He gave a courteous nod and waited nervously for what would come next.

"Follow me, you have been reassigned," he was informed, and the man spun on his heel and headed for the kennel door to escape the stench of the battle hounds. Jasper, a squat man of about forty years, left his present company without uttering a word. The other men returned to their duties as if Mr Thompson had not existed.

As he was led across the courtyard, a series of questions were fired at him: How long had he served in the army of conscripts? How long had he worked in the kennels? Where was his family? The answers: four years, three years this coming October in the kennels, and he had no family due to the raids in the north. Jasper wanted to know about the man asking all these questions, but he offered no information. He stopped abruptly, causing Jasper to clatter into his back, as he was following so closely.

The uniformed man turned, unaggrieved, and said, "You have been given a great opportunity, Jasper Thompson, remember where your loyalties lie, and you will be fine."

He began walking again, finally coming to rest at the largest white waggon. Rapping politely on the door, he stepped back. The door swung open and out stepped Fuldus. Jasper instantly bowed and fell to one knee.

"Get up, Mr Thompson," came his master's voice. "You, I understand, are familiar with the child Little Death, are you not?"

Where was this line of questioning going? he wondered. "Yes, sir, she visits the hounds often," he responded.

"I am also informed that you make her feel at ease. Coupled with the fact that you served bravely in the army." Fuldus paused, pleasantries were not his strongest suit and the exercise was becoming somewhat tiresome. "Coupled with that," he repeated, as if to regain his school of thought, "I am to appoint you Little Death's personal escort."

Jasper raised his head and boomed, "It will be my honour, sir, I will protect her with my life!"

Fuldus was taken aback by the small man's gusto. "That is good, my friend, because fail her and that is exactly what you will pay with," he countered and with that, climbed back into the waggon and closed the door.

Jasper barely had time to run to the armoury and collect a short sword, his dagger, a side arm, musket, shot, powder, body armour and helmet, before he was seated next to the driver as the waggon began to trundle towards the slowly opening citadel gates.

The ocean of people in the marketplace instantly began to clear a path. Anyone not moving quickly enough was shoved aside by the foot soldiers at the head of the procession, two dozen of them armed to the teeth and ferocious looking to boot. Following them was the first waggon, a troop carrier, with twelve more men inside. The infantrymen would alternate; every three hours, the twelve walking would be replaced by those in the waggon. Three hours marching followed by three hours rest. Behind that was the white waggon, the only occupants were Fuldus and his Little Death.

She could not help but steal a peep through the soft red cotton curtains that covered the open windows. The inside of the carriage was already warm, and the open windows let in the air but kept out the summer bugs which proliferated on the banks of the Thames.

This was the first time Beth could remember being outside of the walls of the citadel. Everything was as new and as exciting as a birthday present. She had never seen so many people in one place. The market was now heaving and at its busiest. The cries of traders, the haggling of customers, the singing buskers, the juggling clowns and the tumbling jesters—it all looked so much more fun than the stuffy party she had attended. She could see the sunlight glittering off the water below, the cries of the gulls circling overhead made her look to the blue skies.

The smell of livestock, not unlike the smell of the battle hound enclosure, the bleating, the braying and the clucking, a symphony of noise was everywhere. Each stall she saw was as different from the one before it as it was from the one that followed it. Striped canopies red, white, blue and yellow. Some with the names of the goods they were selling. Fresh farm eggs, said one, the finest beef from Kent, another cheese and cream.

The clatter of pots and pans bouncing off the cobble stone in a two-wheeled barrow, mixed with a lilting tune played on a penny whistle. The scent of fresh bread, pastries, flowers, vegetables, animals, people, sweat and garbage, it was almost overwhelming. Just as her head was beginning to spin, she noticed an old woman standing amongst a display of strawberries. Her attention came back into focus. The old woman had something in her hand. Before Beth could discover what it was, the woman threw her hand into the air and a snow-white dove fluttered free. Beth's eyes followed it until the sun blinded her for a second and the bird was gone.

The cortege of waggons had crossed the market and was now leaving the bridge. The soldiers at the front continued to clear a path and eventually the waggons joined the road on the other side of the river. Beth craned her head back to take a last lingering look at the hubbub of the market. How she wished she could run wild like the many children in the square. *That was never likely to happen, but one day, maybe,* she thought.

The interior of the waggon was cooler now, a steady breeze making the curtains on the windows flutter and dance.

Fuldus was travelling backwards, sitting facing Beth. His eyelids were becoming heavy, and his head nodded back and forth with the rhythm of the waggon's movement across the cobbled streets.

"Like a giant baby being rocked to sleep," Beth smilingly whispered to herself. The view from the window was very different now, less people and more shadows. Some of the smaller lanes and alleyways were quite ominous looking. People scuttled in and out of doorways as she slowly passed.

From above where the driver was sitting, Beth could hear a voice shout at a dog to, "Clear off!" She looked but she could not see it. She knew it was there from its high-pitched yapping, and eventual yelp and then silence. Beth pulled her head back inside the window and for the first time, really looked at the inside of the white waggon. The seats, which ran from wall to wall, were roughly twenty feet in width. They were covered in the softest white leather, with red velvet buttons sunk into them. The leather cushioning continued up onto the walls, though it was not as plush. Above her head was a bunk bed with gold lace curtains, which were tied back with red satin tassels. This, Beth assumed, was to be hers, as she doubted the weight of Fuldus would stay on such a flimsy shelf for long.

Where Fuldus was seated was a mirror image, except instead of a bed, there were four cupboards. The doors nearest the windows were solid and painted white. The doors in the middle were glass in white frames, all had golden handles. Through the glass, Beth could make out the silhouettes of cups hanging on hooks, dancing to the same rhythm as Fuldus' head. At the centre of the waggon, hanging from the ceiling by a sturdy gilt chain, was a square lantern. Within it were six unlit candles. It also swung back and forth as they continued to journey out of the city towards the countryside.

Beth had never seen so much greenery; fields and trees in the fullest of summer foliage dazzled in the bright sunlight. The scents of wildflowers filling the air. Birdsong accompanied the ever-present creak of the waggons and the hollow clopping of the horses. In the distance, Beth could see a field dappled with black and white cows and further off, the sails of a windmill. Water gushing told of the approach to a river. Beth laughed to herself at the sudden lurch in her stomach as they crossed the small hump-backed bridge that spanned it. She was lost in daydreams, the perfumed air cooling her face, her eyes half closed, making the shapes of hills and trees dissolve and vanish.

A sudden "Whoa!" from above took her by surprise, and the waggon juddered to a halt.

Fuldus, who until this time had been silent to the point of invisibility, was instantly alert and on his feet. "Why have we stopped?" he called.

"Infantry change and water for the horses, sir," came the reply. Beth stood also and opening the door, jumped down to the yellow dirt road. The city had vanished, *I must have fallen asleep*, she thought as Fuldus stepped down behind her. He raised his arms above his head and stretched as he did. This was the first time Beth had seen the whole column of vehicles. Behind the white waggon were a pantry waggon and an armoury. Behind that were a dozen fresh horses, a mixture of greys and chestnut browns.

Beth surveyed the crowd of people falling from various doors and jumping down from waggon roofs. She recognised none, until Emma emerged from the pantry with a bundle of bread and cheese wrapped in a red and white chequered tablecloth. She approached Fuldus, "Shall I prepare you a light meal, my lord?" she enquired.

Fuldus gave a nod, a blanket was quickly spread and the food put out. The bread was warm from the sun, and the cheese sweating, crumbled easily. Emma peeled and sliced some apples and fanned the pieces out on a square-shaped wooden plate. To all intents and purposes, they appeared to be a perfectly ordinary family enjoying an evening picnic.

Fuldus leaned back on some hastily arranged cushions whilst enjoying the suns warmth on his face. "We will make camp here this evening and move on at first light," he told the guard nearest to him. Tents were soon erected, and sentries positioned to form a perimeter. The brook was satisfying the horses and the trees to the left gave shelter from the sun. The forest beyond was cool, thick and dark. The twisted knots of branches and summer leaves made the interior hard to make out, but birdsongs and cricket calls nonetheless made it look inviting.

As the sun began to set, a fire was lit in the centre of the tents and a flute was being played somewhere out of sight. Beth was at the water's edge bathing her feet, unaware of the many eyes upon her. Fuldus was sitting now in a veritable mountain of cushions and could not help but smile at the simple pleasures on offer; swimming had always been a favoured pastime of his as a child. His eyelids dropped and he was soon drifting to sleep. Emma was nearby also; she was distracted, though, with the chores of repacking the waggon before she would settle to rest.

The fast-running brook was making Beth's toes prune and a cold shiver was passing through her body. The sound of the water was hypnotic, and she found herself relaxing in spite of the chill. The setting sun colouring the glittering ripples transfixed her, as the water coursed over small rocks and stones. She raised her head, suddenly aware of a sound, something like a small door creaking open. As her eyes adjusted to the dimming light, blinking, she tried to focus on what it was she was looking at.

From the trees had stepped four figures. Much taller than herself, gangling and implausibly skinny. From the distance, it was hard to distinguish whether they were young, old, or even men, or women. They looked like nothing Beth had encountered before. They were dressed, if dressed were the correct way to describe how their bodies were covered. Wrapped would be a more fitting description with leather straps bound tightly from their necks down to their feet.

As the figures came closer, Beth could make out ashen faces, shaven heads and long sinuous fingers. They did not so much walk as dance, wandering and waltzing in her direction. Then with terrifying speed, they began to dart towards her. Beth's initial curious interest in the mummified figures was rapidly being replaced with alarm. The wet ground on which she was sitting did not want to let her quickly stand, sucking at her clothes as she attempted to do so. Her bare feet were slipping on the slick grass as she tried to push away from the onrushing figures.

Their shadows were already upon her as she turned towards the camp. Cold talon-like hands clawed her shoulders before she could call out, lifting her from the ground and turning her to face their owners. Piercing blue eyes, thin red lips, a woman's face, scarred, with none of the tenderness of Emma's. The lips parted to speak, revealing teeth filed to points, each studded with alternate rubies and emeralds. The tip of the woman's nose brushed Beth's, her sour breath filled her head, and then an instruction in a barely audible voice. "Scream," she hissed.

Beth tried to wriggle free but now at least three pairs of hands had her secure. She craned her head towards the camp, which was now receding, the woman was heading towards the trees from whence she had come.

"Scream," came the silent order again. This time, Beth found the air within her lungs and duly obliged.

A terrified siren wail filled the evening twilight. All in the convoy were to their feet in an instant. "Beth," said Emma to herself, "Beth, Beth!" She cried as she headed towards the sound of the disembodied howling.

Fuldus bolted upright scattering cushions as he did, his eyes scanning the growing darkness. He frantically peered around and finally; he saw the figures on the other side of the brook. Guards were already crashing across the water as Beth and her abductors vanished into the protective dark of the forest.

No sooner had the four who had carried Beth away vanished from sight, four more stepped into view. The heavily armed men paused momentarily before forging onward. The figures raised their arms in front of them, each hand holding a small and beautifully crafted crossbow pistol. Deadly accurate were each of them, the bolts flew and the first six of the men fell writhing in agony as the bolts made their homes in kneecaps and hard skulls. Battle hounds had been loosed, and they ploughed with no sense of fear into the trees. Fuldus was now down by the water's edge and could clearly hear the whizzing of more bolts and the whimper of the mighty dogs as each was cut down. By now, twenty men were hacking at the tangle of branches impeding their advance. As they moved natures thorny fingers ripped at them, snagging clothes and skin alike.

Fuldus was now there with them slicing a clearance with his broadsword; the foliage parted, and the men found themselves engulfed by the darkness of the trees. There was, however, more than enough light to fight or make chase. Each looked at the other, helpless—what now? Then it came, another scream, distant and muffled. Fuldus was the first to react and charged in the direction of the sound. He was becoming increasingly concerned though, he could hear her but could not see where she and her captors were.

Fuldus raised his hand and all in the party stopped. He craned his head; blasts of air escaped his nostrils as he waited for another sign as to the direction in which Little Death was being taken. Silence, not even the birds were disturbed. Then the fizz of crossbow bolts and the howls of those at the rear of the party crashing to the ground. Bodies were falling like skittles, some pulling barbed missiles from their wounds. Those left standing formed a circle, ready to repel whatever attack may come next, but none did. There were a few moments of silence, eager eyes surveying the immediate landscape. Nothing, no sound, no movement, no attack. Little Death and the apparitions that had taken her had vanished.

Fuldus craned his head, becoming increasingly more frantic. His few remaining guards stood ready but not knowing for what. A scream from the north sliced through the silence, a piercing, terrified scream. Fuldus lunged ahead, and even without uttering a command, his men were at his back, weapons ready.

Another scream, but still no one was visible amongst the thickening trees and darkness. Again silence, except for heavy breaths and grinding of teeth.

The air was suddenly alive, as if a swarm of angry metallic bees had just left their hive; soft thuds of the tiny objects striking tree trunks were soon joined by cries of men, as whizzing, slicing, razor sharp stars began finding softer targets. Eyes and cheeks, thighs and hands, giant men felled by the tiniest of weapons. Fuldus reacted to a flash of light, raising his sword just in time to send a flying star ricocheting to safety. Like snowflakes driven on the cruellest winter wind, they came in clouds, the only escape was to dive flat to the ferns and thorns of the forest floor.

Fuldus was now isolated but still trying to reach the fading screams. A wall of ivy hung before him; a slick green curtain almost as black as the night. His sword made light work of it, revealing a clearing that looked like a lightning strike had created it. Trees were nothing but stumps and charcoal. The smell of smouldering and soot were still fresh.

The grass that remained was blackened and charred. Fuldus stamping amongst it, raised small clouds of fine grey ash. His eyes were becoming used to the dim twilight. The trees surrounding him appeared to have a life of their own, but as the dust cleared and settled, Fuldus found he was actually in a thicket of the oddest creatures he had ever seen tall and lithe, deathly pale and now screaming like banshees. Sword in hand they tumbled like circus acrobats. One rushed toward him somersaulting over his head, causing him to drop to one knee, positioning his sword horizontally to protect his skull from the downward thrust of a short sword. He leapt to his feet as they passed above him, sending them crashing to the ground, but with catlike grace and speed, they were upright in the blink of an eye.

He pulled a dagger from his belt and held it at full stretch, and in his other hand was his broadsword. Slowly, he turned on the spot, trying to gauge how many people were surrounding him, expecting to be engulfed in the same wave of savagery which had already removed his companions. The silence now, was more unsettling than the bloodcurdling screams of moments before, and it was partly because of this he chose to speak.

"You have taken something of mine, something precious and I mean for it to be returned." A response of hisses and cackles. "Where have you taken the child?" he continued. "Answer me, damn you!" he bellowed.

Crows roosting in the nearby trees filled the sky, invisible except for the harshest of cries. A mist of murmuring whisked around him, nothing made sense, it was like listening to a dozen conversations taking place in another room. One voice then became clear, a serpentine voice, soft and feminine. "We of the order of Vengeance do not answer to the false king," it seethed.

The statement was met by more hissing and whispered mocking repetition, "False king, false king, false king."

It was then Fuldus realised he was in fact surrounded by women, women who had achieved something no force of men had managed in all the years he could recall, that being the defeat of a party of hill tribesmen.

These women were clearly not to be underestimated. Fuldus was aware though, the longer he stood there in conversation, the further Little Death was moving from him. "Don't believe for one second your sex will stop me from cutting you all down," he said stamping his feet and making dust rise once more. "You will meet the same end as your Brothers," he laughed aloud. "I assume it was they who sent you," he added coldly. All the time he spoke, he continued turning on the spot, counting those around him. Seven. "Your sly weapons will not stop me," his bravado was returning. "You will gain nothing but a swift end in the dead grass under an indifferent sky." His sense of invincibility that was briefly shaken was also returning; he began to strut like an actor awaiting applause. "Now, be good nuns and return the child to me." He looked at each of them. Pallid faces atop creaking, coiled bodies, poised to spring at any moment, mewing, whining and growling back at him. It was now or never.

"So be it," he said in an almost matter-of-fact way, "You leave me…" but before he could finish his sentence, a blade sped towards him, grazing his ear. The cold sting awakened something deep within him, something that he thought was no longer there: fear.

It unleashed him, releasing him from what little conscience he had about butchering women; he became a whirling surgeon, each of his incisions piercing the right organ, severing the correct artery, amputating a limb. Moments had passed, the clearing was once again a blizzard of ash, the moon, the only witness to the night's events. Fuldus was unharmed. The Sisters of Vengeance now had seven less members.

The roar of blood rushing through his veins began to subside, his thinking becoming more settled and clearer. His eyes darted left and right. He slowed his breathing and listened, standing in silence for what seemed like an eternity. Then a cry, was it a fox or an owl? There it was again. Once more he was charging into the dark tapestry of the forest. Any demon prowling the woods that night would have thought twice before standing in his way. A dry branchless tree stump crashed to the ground under the force of his momentum.

He had crossed a mile when he left the trees behind him and found himself bearing down on a small wooden cabin, more like a shed. *One good gust of wind would level it,* he thought. Without breaking stride, his shoulder splintered the door and he was inside. The room was barely ten feet square and seemingly empty. Panic again ambushed him.

Had he been led astray? Had his quarry doubled back taking Little Death with them, were they now making a getaway in the opposite direction? Could he have been that easily fooled? He quietly cursed himself at the thought.

He surveyed the room. Streaks of light seeped through the walls from the outside. There were two small windows. One no more than a square hole, the other dust-coated glass pathetically dressed in a faded red cotton curtain. But the room made no sense to him. With the door gone and a non-existent window welcoming the night air, why was this place so unnaturally warm?

Fuldus shifted his feet, moving weight from one to the other, creaks and groans answered, the wood barely able to support his frame. Then like a child about to bounce on a trampoline, bending his knees he jumped and brought both feet to the floor at once with a thud. Again, this time with more force, and again. The shack was shuddering. He vaulted one more time, his head grazing its rafters as he did, this time when he landed the floor gave way beneath him.

He landed on his feet in a tiny passage, his own weight forcing him to drop to his haunches, but he forced himself upright immediately. The floor was raw soil as were the walls, which were too close to draw his sword. His shoulders scarcely had the room to navigate their confines. He drew his dagger once more and held it before him.

The heat in the narrow tunnel was almost overpowering. It was pitch dark apart from a shaft of light up ahead. He shuffled towards it with as much caution as the setting allowed. When he reached it, the tunnel turned sharply, and the space opened up before him. The floor beneath his feet was now flagstones. The heat was being generated by a large raging fire, fed by a pair of bellows some ten feet in width and being operated by a scrawny wretch, whose eyes were bound as if she was blind. Consequently, she seemed oblivious to Fuldus' approach.

Behind the fire was a wooden wall with a door located centrally. *None of it was built to withstand an assault,* he thought. He continued to inch forwards, the door now his objective. *If a place was so surreptitiously constructed, it must have a purpose,* he thought. His instinct was to dramatically stamp his feet to bring any unseen occupants of the rooms beyond the wall to him, but before he had time to put his plan into action, the seemingly blind bellows operator began to wail like a cat, phlegm rattling in her throat, her skeletal jaw hardly moving, the catcalls slowly transformed into words, "Out, out, out! He is here, my Sisters, the orphan boy!" Her wails fell silent and she replaced them with a deliberate guttural cackling, "the false king is here," she hissed, "the soon dead king is here."

The fire's attendant fell silent once more. Fuldus had heard her words, but concentrating as he was on the door, paid her no real heed. Hoards would soon engulf him, he waited but there was nothing; the door remained closed. He continued his advance, albeit tentatively. He was there now gripping its handle, and then inhaling deeply, sprang into the unknown space beyond. Still nothing, no spinning razors, no howling she-witches, just silence, the smell of soil and the over baring heat.

This room, though, was darker than the previous one, but Fuldus could still make out a lone figure standing in the shadows. He steeled himself for the inevitable attack, but again nothing.

He kept his knife before him, the lack of aggression was more tortuous than the earlier onslaught. He began to inch forwards, his eyes now unravelling the dark to reveal another member of the sisterhood. The same leather bindings over translucent skin, pale lips moving as if in silent prayer. Still she made no movement despite his obvious approach.

Fuldus darted his powerful arm before him, grasping the woman by the throat. Her eyes flickered, then slowly, disdainfully opened. No fear was evident in her non-blinking stare. Fuldus could feel her life slipping away, but she would be no good to him dead even though that was preferable to him. "Where is the child?" he whispered as he loosened his grip in the hope of an answer.

She inhaled, her lips parting just enough to reveal her filed teeth. He could feel the bones in her neck slide beneath his grip and her jaw move as she tried to speak. He released her further but kept his blade at her stomach. "The child is lost to you," she whispered. Fuldus was appalled at the thought, and the sister could see it in his eyes. She greeted it with a sneer and continued, "Lost to you, just like your mother and your sister."

He closed his fist again, lifting her a few inches from the ground, but her rasping goading continued, "The gods offer you their protection, they would have been better off giving it to any of them," she laughed, "you can save no one." Her body began to dance in his grasp, the last of her laughter wheezed from her body as she slumped to the floor.

As she fell, she became entangled in a filthy curtain which was directly behind her. The brass rings holding it in place on a slender rail popped one by one, and as the curtain fell it revealed a wooden staircase seemingly heading back up to the surface. A cool breeze greeted Fuldus as he stepped over his fallen tormentor. The top of the stairs now visible, lit by the moon. He forced his way up, loosing soil and stones as he went.

Clear of the stairs and once more in the open air, he instantly drew his sword. Filling his lungs and quickly scanning the area, his eyes settled on a covered waggon. His presence unsettled the four powerful black horses tethered to it. Snorting and stamping, they alerted the comparatively diminutive figures next to them.

This must be where they were readying their escape. "Beth!" he roared, and not waiting for a reply he charged towards the waggon. In an instant, the cracking of a whip set the four horses in motion and hurtling directly towards him. Fuldus stopped in his tracks, his eyes desperately searching for some advantage, but nothing offered itself. Sword in hand, he fell to the left and swung his blade at full stretch, catching the nearest horse above the fetlock as it careered past. The unfortunate beast instantly collapsed and dragged the other three horses with it, spinning the waggon over before it landed upright in a tangled heap of muscle, canvas and splintering wood.

The driver of the waggon had been hurled a good thirty feet clear of the wreck and, having collided with a tree, was lying lifeless, presenting no immediate threat. Fuldus approached what was left of the waggon, desperate to see if Beth was inside. The fallen horses neighed and cried out in agony, masking any sound that may be coming from inside. He was within arm's reach of the back curtains when a clearly injured Sister lunged through them, shrieking past him she landed in a bloodied pile, face down on the ploughed earth beneath.

He slid the toe of his boot under her shoulder and flipped her body over. His eyes met hers, open, blank, staring and apparently dead. Stepping over her, he was now inside the ruin of the waggon. Debris was strewn within; no other bodies were visible. If Beth was inside, had she been thrown clear, lying injured nearby? Fuldus forced his way back through the canvas, calling her name and craning his head in all directions, but nothing.

He was trying not to believe he had been duped into following a decoy, but it was seeming more likely. Now in the distance, he could hear his own name being called. The remnants of his guards belatedly coming to his aid. He stepped towards the onrushing crowd, Emma being the first face he recognised closely followed by Jasper Thompson.

Emma could see the panic in his eyes. "My lord," she whispered, reaching her hand towards him, offering and in search of solace.

He threw his head back and released a primal, roaring, anguished scream. Rage at his own inability to protect the girl. His mind painting horrifying pictures of what might await her at the hands of the Sisters of Vengeance. He could barely control himself. "Spread out!" he barked, "Leave no stone unturned, find her!"

The crowd instantly began to disperse in all directions. Calls of "Beth!" filled the night. Fuldus dropped to his haunches and slowed his breathing. He was momentarily a small boy, the rain soaking him to his skin, weeping for his dead mother and the sister he never knew.

The search party was already leaving silence in their wake. Fuldus was forcing himself to stand when a sound behind him snapped him back to reality. He instinctively had his sword tip to the fallen sister, using it to turn her body again. She was still dead, as far as he could see. The sound came again, muffled but distinct. It was coming from inside the wrecked waggon. Taking the hem of the tattered canvas in both hands, he tore it away like flesh from a cadaver, revealing its broken ribs.

Still there were no signs of life, but there it was again, this time more frantic. Again, and again it came. Fuldus began pulling at bales of clothes and baskets of rags, the wreck was suddenly enveloped by flying canvas, fluttering and twisting like bats in the night sky.

Fuldus clawed at the once orderly contents of the waggon, sending them in all directions. He grazed his knuckles on the raw wood planks that comprised the floor, then pressing his palms flat against them, he waited. There, it came again, a knocking sending vibrations through his body.

He cleared the immediate area of the floor, sweeping out from the centre to the sides. His left hand sliding over refreshingly cold metal hinges, his right finding a loop of rough rope. He leaned back. He was looking at a small door, about three feet by two in size, a smuggler's secret cupboard no doubt.

Taking the rope handle in both hands he pulled with such a force as to send the door spinning into the air, the knocking immediately ceased. Beneath him, now he could see the terrified eyes of a gagged and bound Little Death.

He scooped her up, vainly trying to control his own emotions. Her tiny body vanished into the cavernous folds of his arms. "I thought you were gone," he whispered. Then releasing her gag, held her at arm's length before him, "Are you injured?" he asked, his eyes darting over her from head to toe looking for obvious signs of damage. He could see none, then craning his head, he roared, "Emma," into the darkness behind him.

As gently as his stinging hands would allow, he loosened her bonds. He controlled his breathing, composing himself, so no one would see the signs of the humanity he had briefly displayed. Calls were behind him now as the search party began racing back to the crashed waggon. He stepped from the wreckage, cradling the still silent Beth. Emma was the first to them, Fuldus passed Beth to her without saying a word. He then strolled past her and headed back to the caravan, as if he had merely been taking in the cool night air.

The journey back to Fulham though was an urgent and frantic affair. Any romantic thoughts Fuldus had entertained about a grand tour of his kingdom were now a distant memory. The horses were not allowed to stop for breath nor water. If the Brotherhood had any other plans to attack, Fuldus knew his party was now dangerously vulnerable.

One waggon was full of the injured, lame, blind and those near death. Fuldus sat in isolation in his own carriage. Those still capable of bearing arms were riding within the armoury waggon, where Emma and Beth had spent the remains of the night sleeping under heavy guard. Six men clung to the roof and two more kept watch from the tailboards. The sun had risen hours ago, and the day was now warm, the interior of the waggon so crowded was humid and stinking. Emma had moved Beth to the bench seat to get fresh air from the arrow slit windows. Beth's unblinking eyes did not seem to register even the sun.

The caravan charged on, the noise of the road beneath its wheels changing from the crushing of dried earth to the clatter of wood and iron on cobblestones. Fulham was now only minutes away. The narrow streets were alive with the usual bustle. The call went through the streets, the news of Fuldus' return reaching the gates of the citadel quicker than the horses could negotiate the crowded city. Two riders left the bridge in front of the main gates, clearing a path for the approaching waggons. The gates were slowly opening, a wooden mouth in a stone face waiting to swallow the onrushing horses.

The market vendors scrambled to clear carts and goods from the main thoroughfare. One stall toppled and spilled Granny Smith's and Conference pears to the floor. A melee ensued as a free meal was sensed by the street urchins, who gravitated to the market looking for easy pockets to pick or anything that was easily pilfered, to be sold later in the beggar's market in Blackfriars.

A small crowd was still in the middle of the bridge when the leading waggon began to race towards the safety of the citadel gates. The driver was in no mood to stop, his eyes narrow, concentrating on keeping control of the exhausted horses. The first he knew of the crowd in his path was the screams of those watching as he ploughed towards them.

Instinctively, he pulled with all his strength to halt the four horses. They obliged as best they could, but weight of the waggon continued to propel it forwards, making it swing wildly to the right, colliding with Missus Issitt's kitchen supply stall. Copper pots and pans were launched skywards, shouts and screams accompanied them, and now a cacophony of falling kitchenware added to the discord. The second waggon ground to a halt, narrowly avoiding smashing into the first.

A crowd materialised as if from nowhere, a frenzy of grabbing, tug-o-war, howling and fighting. Guards were now streaming from the citadel, trying to clear a path but just adding to the mayhem. The scene was rapidly descending into riot.

Fuldus pushed his head past the curtain covering his window. "What the hell is going on up there?" he roared. Emma was now on the street, standing on tiptoes to get a better look. One of the tribesmen with a view from the roof shouted back a report of the disturbance in the market.

Fuldus jumped down and began shoving past people trying to leave the bridge. He was swimming against the tide, but his progress was rapid. Emma realised they were not going to make it back to safety unless they were on foot. She reached her hand into the waggon and pulled Beth towards her. Fuldus was soon at her shoulder.

"Get these people out of the way," he ordered his men.

They sprang to action; bodies were flying left to the pavements and bouncing off the waggons to the right. The guards from the citadel were preforming the same action from the other side of the crowd. Between them, they had soon cleared a corridor for Emma to carry Beth unhindered.

Fuldus and his party were now clear of the mob. Emma stumbled, two guards rushed towards her and kept her upright. Emma thanked them and asked Beth to walk the remaining few yards but did not let go of her hand for a second. Fuldus turned and looked disdainfully at the scene in the marketplace. He beckoned to the captain of the watch, "Restore order here." He began to walk away as the guards formed a human wall to press the crowd back and off the bridge.

Scores of people were still fighting as the men advanced, pushing and trampling on those who did not have the sense to retreat. The crowd had already been pushed some thirty feet from Fuldus; as a result, the calmer side of the bridge was clear except for a small dishevelled man who was pulling himself to his feet.

Fuldus, finally turning away, shook his head. "Disgraceful," he muttered to himself. Emma and the few remaining guards looked on bemused. "Everyone, inside," said Fuldus as he prepared to leave the now quiet bridge. Rain was beginning to fall on the city and thunder rumbled in the distance. The gates were being readied to close when a shout came from behind him.

"My lord! A moment please." Fuldus stopped as did everyone else. "My lord!" came the call again as heads began to turn. Standing there on his own was the man who moments before had pulled himself from the ground.

Fuldus took a step towards him. "What do you want?" he snapped. The man theatrically dusted himself down and straightened the rather scruffy blue neckerchief he was wearing and gave a very courteous bow that drew smiles and chuckles from those watching.

"My lord," he repeated, "I bring a message." He took a step towards Fuldus whilst removing a small object from his pocket. "A message from the Brotherhood of the Light for the false king." As he was talking, he raised his hand, and before anyone could react, fired a single shot from a small pistol.

The sound was barely audible over the falling rain and distant thunder. Fuldus jolted and stumbled backwards a few steps, his hands instinctively clasping his chest. His men flew past him towards the shabby gunman. They piled on top of him, no more shots were fired. Fuldus looked down and raised his palms towards him. Clean, no blood. He checked his arms, turned his head left and right, nothing. He was unharmed.

His guards now had the much smaller man in their custody. The rain was running down his unremarkable face, soaking the rough linen shirt he wore. He did not struggle, standing stock-still. Fuldus allowed a triumphant "Ha!" to explode from his lungs. "Are you the best your masters could hire?" he mocked. "Bring him inside, we have much to discuss." Fuldus was gleeful at the thought of what the news of his assassin's failure would do to the Keeper of the Secrets. Smiling, he turned away.

Emma was still standing in the same place, shocked and bemused by what had just happened. She looked to Beth whose hand had slipped from hers. Their eyes met. Beth's lips parted as if she was to speak for the first time that day. No sound, no words. "What is it, my love?" asked Emma softly. Beth swallowed and as she did, a small stream of blood trickled from the corner of her mouth.

Emma leaned back to get a better view of the child standing beside her. The line of blood traced a course to the side of her chin and continued down her neck to her collarbone, gathering speed as it went. Beth dropped to her knees. Fuldus looked on, not knowing what to make of it. The front of Beth's dress clung to her tiny frame, soaked with rain and blood. The gods may have spared Fuldus; the bullet, however, was not so generous.

Beth had been shot in the chest. Emma, screaming and sobbing, caught her as she was about to keel forwards to the cold stone of the bridge. Beth was hanging in her arms like a sodden rag doll. Fuldus was on them, dragging Emma to her feet. Calls were ringing around the stone walls for the surgeon. Fuldus gently turned Beth towards him and put his ear to her mouth, he could hear nothing.

The doctor had arrived, almost immediately applying pressure to the wound to stem the bleeding, and with that, they were gone to the infirmary. The assassin was now singing at the top of his voice, a song heralding the return of the Brotherhood. One of the guards drew his dagger and within an instant had the blade to his throat. Fuldus turned to them. "No!" he bellowed, "Alive! I want him alive." He wanted the man dead. He had never wanted to kill a man so desperately in his entire life.

The rage inside him was almost uncontrollable. Rage at the assassin, rage at the bullet, rage at himself again for not protecting the child. The bullet was meant for him, if only he had known he would have welcomed it. Taken it to his own heart and held it there like a long-lost loved one.

The now silent man was thrown at Fuldus' feet. "Take," he finished his sentence with a sneer, "that to the cells, make sure no harm comes to him." The man in the blue neckerchief was dragged across the wet stones. Fuldus smiled at him, yelling as he vanished into the citadel, "You and I are about to become very closely acquainted my friend!" and with that he was gone. The bridge was finally cleared, and the doors to the citadel closed. The night now dark, wet, and thunderous, was left with the chore of washing Beth's blood from the cobbles and the memory of the day.

The Old Man

The city bustled about its daily business. *Ankles,* thought the old man, *I see no faces, just boots in dust, or mud and puddles.* He would sit during daylight hours with his hands outstretched, hoping for whatever small coins would come his way. He would sit at night also, in rain and wind. In the heat of summer and the bone-chilling raw pain of winter.

He would sometimes put words into the mouth of the growling empty sounds his stomach would make. "When did the world change?" it would ask him. "How did we end up here?" He would remind his empty stomach that life was not always this way. "We were happy once, I was father, husband, happy!" he would shout. The ankles would continue to kick up dust or splash past him paying no heed.

He would remember his life and the joy of his children but could not remember the last time he spoke with them. He could remember their faces neither, let alone the last time he laid eyes upon them. Maybe they were just ankles now. Ankles with their heads on back to front as they marched by.

He could still feel the joy of his wife. Remembering her death felt like acid burning inside him. There was a house, he would smile to himself at the thought. It was small, and pretty. Just like his wife. There was a garden, flowers would be cut and placed on a dinner table. Vegetables were grown and cooked and served with love. There was love, he remembered it. He would howl like a dog in pain at its loss.

Coins would bounce next to him as the ankles rushed past. He would scrabble to collect them before they were kicked from his reach. He was a teacher, he remembered. Eager minds listened to him; now he was just a body, discarded, forgotten, hands outstretched looking for coins.

His head buzzed most days with the voices and the screams of the city, the constant questions from his stomach and the pain in his limbs. How much longer could he live in fear? How many days, weeks, years had he been alone? Why did no one see him? Had he become invisible? Was he becoming nothing? Was he now alive only in his own memory? Were the coins falling from above, not meant for him at all? Was he literally stealing pennies from heaven to keep himself on the earth? His head was spinning, almost out of control. He looked to his trembling hands and bit down on his knuckles to assure himself he wasn't a bodyless spectre. A voice, not one his own soothed him. Was there still someone listening? For a second he was home, his family around him, happy.

With a long absent smile on his face he stretched his fingers to their fullest length, until his sinews hurt, and his joints popped, and then he forced his hands into the earth.

The Question

The remaining hours of the day passed more slowly than anyone had ever experienced. Each second gave all who had witnessed the events of that afternoon time to reflect, imagine alternative scenarios that would have ended less horrifically. Fuldus over and again hearing the taunts of the Sisterhood, unable to protect yet another person he...he should not even think of the word, but there it was again, love. Had his feelings for the child somehow angered the Oracle? Had he reneged on their agreement? Was he being punished? Was the only person in his world that he did indeed have feelings for to be taken from him, because unknown to himself he had broken their secret pact?

He could bear it no longer, the questions were driving him to insanity. All thoughts of revenge were gone, for now at least, swept away by a tide of regret. He found himself standing outside the surgeon's quarters. A small crowd was milling about the hallway. All eyes were on him. Could they see his guilt? Did they sense his betrayal? Did they see his weakness? Did they feel as he did, that this was his fault, his punishment?

He stood in silence, trying to look nonchalant. Emma half-stepped to him, anguish etched on her face, her eyes away in some distant place where she had already buried her beloved Beth. "There is no news," was all she could muster in way of comfort as the hours crept on.

The torches had almost burned down, their light and warmth being replaced by the early morning sun. Fuldus had not moved, he would watch from his safe distance as Emma had all that night, sat on a rough wooden bench, drifting in and out of flashback-filled dreams which would instantly waken her to the reality of waiting.

The numbers in the halls grew and shrank intermittently as the day progressed. It was now approaching noon; the surgeon's door had remained firmly closed since Beth was carried in there some eighteen hours earlier. Fuldus was beginning to think that the men charged with her care, having lost the fight to save her, were too terrified to come out and tell him. He formed a fist and was about to thump the door and demand some news, but the chance of doing more damage than good restrained him. He closed his eyes and exhaled slowly, as he opened them again, the surgeon's door had silently opened.

Doctor James Hart looked exhausted as he stepped into the hallway. He was a small man in his sixties and the expectation of success was obviously weighing heavily upon him. He cleared his throat, "My lord, the girl lives," those assembled released a unified sigh of relief, the doctor though needed to temper their expectations and added, "but barely, luckily the bullet did not enter her heart." Fuldus listened intently, as the doctor continued, "She has lost a lot of blood and is breathing very shallowly." Hart took a swig from a small hip flask before continuing. "I successfully removed the bullet, but she is so frail I fear the worst."

Muffled gasps and sobbing from Emma replaced the fleeting sense of optimism. "My lord, the next few hours will be crucial, I suggest the girl's maid stay with her, talk to her, and try and keep her from crossing over." With that, he buckled at the knees. Having been on feet for nearly a day and a half, he was near to collapse. Fuldus caught his elbow, "I am sorry, my lord, there is nothing else I can do." He steadied himself and continued, "Had the bullet struck you, my lord, it would have bounced off, it was tiny."

Emma pushed her way into the room while the doctor was still talking, "If only she were older, or a man, I could have done more."

Fuldus had stopped listening. "Go and rest," he said quietly, knowing there was no more to be achieved.

Doctor Hart shuffled away, "If only older and stronger, I could have done more," he repeated as he went, and with that, the door to his chamber closed softly behind him.

Fuldus looked nervously towards the open door wherein lay Beth. He craned his head left and right, surveying those assembled. "Go about your business," his voice was almost inaudible, "Go!"

The small crowd dissolved instantly. Then slowly drawing a deep breath, he stepped into the room. Beth was lying on a bed big enough for twenty children her size, covered only in a white linen sheet. Emma was holding her hand, chattering lightly as if nothing had happened, recounting the details of the room, the weather, anything that would keep her from the truth of the situation.

"Dream, little one," she said softly, "dream of that beautiful garden you told me about." She sniffed back a tear. "It will keep you safe until you return to me."

Fuldus gazed at her briefly, beside the bed was a small table with a bowl of water and a towel. He reached down and dipped the cloth into the lemon-scented water and as softly as a man of his size could, dabbed her forehead. He dislodged her fringe and try as he might, he could not put it right with his clumsy fingers. He placed the towel back on the table and saying nothing, left the room.

He knew the time had come. The Brotherhood were becoming bolder with every passing day. He must act now. If he could find out where the Keeper of the Secrets was holed up, he could smother him in his sleep. If he knew where he would be in a week, a month, or a year. If he only knew when best to launch an attack and slaughter his supporters and allies, but where were they? Who were they? He needed to know, and whatever he was to do, needed to be done soon. His pace quickened, up narrow spiral stairwells, along corridors and before he was even aware of it, he found himself standing before the Oracle.

He was shocked by her appearance. Grey and decaying, like a shadow draped over a winter landscape. Fuldus had made her as comfortable as possible, moving her to a room with a view over the river. She had much appreciated the sunlight of which she had been long starved, but the pain in which she lived daily was ever present and increasingly unbearable.

Fuldus fell to his knees at her bedside, he reached to take her hand, not sure if he could even hold it. Her translucent skin appeared as mist, but cartilage, gristle and bone he could feel in his gentle grasp. "I have come with so many questions," he said as resolutely as he could. "I just need a moment to…" But before he could finish, her hand slipped from his and came to rest on his head. He gritted his teeth to stifle a sob. He was transported to a time long ago when his mother would calm him by doing the same thing.

He looked to her, his eyes stinging. His lips moved, she could see heartbreak, and before he uttered a word, the Oracle smiled, knowing what he needed to hear.

"I see the question in your heart," she assured him, "but, it is the one question which gains you no advantage over your enemies."

Fuldus was uneasy at having his thoughts so easily flicked through, like the pages of a book, open for all to read. The room was becoming warm and dazzlingly bright. Before Fuldus now was a woman, young and beautiful. She stepped from the bed and taking Fuldus by the hands, raised him to his feet. He towered over her, but it was he who was in fear and awe. She was glowing, the air in the room filled with the scent of spring flowers, fresh rain and birdsong. Then a sense of calm wrapped him, a calm he had not felt for many years and unprompted, he asked:

"Will the child live?"

A smile ignited the Oracle's face; she was free, she bowed her head and kissed Fuldus' hands. Then stepping back from him, she began to dissolve into autumn leaves and snowflakes, floating and melting until all that remained was her voice.

"Yes," she said, "Yes, Fuldus, the child will live."

Fuldus walked with new purpose, secured in the knowledge Beth would live. Yes, live, not just survive, but live. He found himself outside the cell where the Brotherhood's gunman was being held. The door was flanked by two heavily armed tribesmen, both of whom Fuldus knew by sight. He nodded, and the door was instantly unlocked.

The man was seated on a rather grand-looking high-backed chair. The table in front of him by comparison was rough and simple. It was orderly, though; a pen and ink were in front of him with a neat pile of parchment. Upon seeing Fuldus enter the room, he sat as if to attention, a faint smile on his lips.

Fuldus exploded, his right fist ploughed into his prisoner's face, sending him somersaulting backwards taking the chair and table with him. The air was alive with sheets of paper circling and gliding, falling like plucked feathers to the floor.

The guards outside rushed in, unsure of what had happened. Fuldus now had the man upright, holding him by his hair, blood flowing freely from his nose; his eyes already bruised and closed from the blow. Fuldus' mouth was at the prisoner's ear. He fired the guards a sharp glance. "Leave us," he hissed. With a modicum of control, he whispered to the prisoner, "I shall harm you no more." Then righting the chair, he dropped the man back onto it. The prisoner slumped back forcing air from his lungs and blowing bubbles of blood from his nostrils.

Fuldus sat him upright and then leaned towards him so their noses practically touched, he continued, "But you, my friend, you will know such pain before you die. The pain you delivered me will be returned a million-fold. Your life will be lived in a state of such agony, you will pray for death, but trust me, it will not come for you; I will see to it the finest most skilled doctors tend to your every need, bring you back to the rudest of health, and then it will begin again with renewed gusto."

Fuldus stood once more, "until I am satisfied you understand what it is you have done. I will fill your veins with hot coal, I will…" he stopped, his teeth grinding, air forcing spittle in the man's face. He was wasting his breath, as all the while the prisoner sat motionless, unmoved by Fuldus and his speech.

He finally composed himself. Sitting opposite his prisoner, he smiled and said, "Let's start with pleasantries, your name, my friend."

The smaller man cleared his throat. "It's Odd," he said. "What's odd?" enquired Fuldus, "The question is odd, or your name is an odd one?" he laughed almost jovially.

"Toliver," the prisoner coughed, "Odd Toliver is my name," came the clarification.

"Yes," said Fuldus, "that is indeed odd." He rose to his feet. "We will not speak again, Mister Toliver," he said abruptly, "But I sincerely hope from now on, you make better decisions than the one that brought you here."

With that, he opened the door, and three other men entered carrying a grim selection of tools and devices. Had one encountered them elsewhere on a different occasion, they might be mistaken for plumbers or carpenters, but certainly not gentlemen. They stopped, awaiting instructions. Fuldus smiled, "Information, pain and information." With that, he left them alone. He was not thirty feet from the cell when the muffled screams began.

Beth's condition did not worsen over the remains of the day, but neither did it improve. Emma stayed by her bedside, taking only a rare sip of water to sustain herself. The situation continued, minutes became hours and hours became days. Beth hovered between this world and whatever may lie beyond. A damp sponge with sugar water was pressed to her lips every hour as per Doctor Hart's instructions. Beth would swallow the tiny amounts of fluid, and this the doctor said was a good thing. Her bleeding had long since ceased and her wound was healing remarkably quickly. Fuldus would listen to these reports but appeared to care not. He knew Beth would be returned to him, it was only a matter of when.

The summer was giving way to the chill of autumn. Fuldus stood at the window of his private chambers, looking longingly at the changing colours of the trees beyond the citadel walls. He had been thinking recently and often of his homeland, the rugged mountains, the rolling hills and lush grasslands. As a boy, he would wander from his caves for days. It was quite normal for hill tribe children to be gone on adventures for weeks at a time, honing skills that would serve them well later in life. He would give a king's ransom in gold to be hunting a bear in the hills and not planning the continued hunt of his enemies.

In his room with him were the commanders of his army, air and sea fleets. Each of his forces was well represented: a commander in chief, a second in command, his assistant, various advisers and intelligence gatherers all milling about trying to make their voices heard. Mister Toliver had been a source of much intelligence. The Brotherhood *had* been the architects of the attempt on Fuldus. They had also forged an alliance with Scandinavians of all people. The same ones who had chased the Keeper and his cohorts into hiding. They planned to invade once more from the north, where Anglia's defences were weakest. The area was completely loyal to Fuldus, and consequently there were very few troops stationed there.

Fuldus had moved quickly. The Brotherhood's spy network in and around the capital had been smashed and those captured were interrogated and put to death. The information gathered all pointed to the same military strategy from the Keeper and his new allies—invasion from the north.

Days before, Fuldus had dispatched his own operatives across the northern sea to confirm the truth of the plans. They had returned hours earlier bringing news that Scandinavian forces were encamped around various ports in Norway, waiting to board three hundred ships. The next new moon would be perfect to make their crossing, the nights were dark and the seas in the north were calmest during early autumn.

In response to the threat, nine out of ten of all garrisons had been sent to make camp in the valleys around Elgin. Sky ships had been flown to higher ground, while the navy was sent along the west coast and around the most northerly tip of the islands to lay in wait.

How would the islanders respond to a new invasion? Fuldus wondered. *Would they welcome the return of the Brotherhood?* They had been loyal to them for decades before his arrival. Surely the people would not dare rebel against him, for fear the invasion would fail and knowing the retaliation that would follow, he reasoned.

The citadel and the south had a minimal number of troops to protect it, but more than enough, Fuldus and his commanders believed, to see off the would-be invaders. He would take one loyal tribesman over ten mercenaries or white-armoured Brothers. They had defeated the Scandic hoard once before from a position much weaker than they were in now. Confidence amongst his forces was high that the outcome would be the same this time.

The gathering of the generals was ending when quite suddenly, the door burst open. This was surprising enough in itself, but what made it more shocking was the sight of Emma hurtling into the room unannounced. Before anyone could speak, she had thrown herself at Fuldus' feet. She was hugging his legs and sobbing.

"My lord, it's a miracle," she muffled. "Our little angel is awake."

Fuldus rapidly cleared the room and dragged Emma to her feet. She had never seen him smile, but he did now. She was probably the first person to see such an event in years, she thought.

"Awake!" he roared. "Where is she?" he paused briefly, "Her old self, is she as she was, is she…"

Emma interrupted, "She woke up, hungry as a horse!" The two of them found themselves walking as quickly as they could without running. Soon they were at her bedside, and sure enough, there she sat, drinking milk and eating cheese and apples.

"Hello, big man," she said with a cheeky smile, "Is the summer over? I want to go to the garden again, you'll be safe there."

Fuldus could not help but look confused by her statement, he looked to Doctor Hart who was standing on the other side of her bed. With no further instruction needed, the doctor spoke. "Well," he began, "it is not unusual for one who has been sleeping so long to confuse dreams with reality upon awaking." He swallowed, "Quite natural, my lord, it will pass in time." With that, the doctor smiled and excused himself.

Fuldus crouched by Beth's bed and took her hand. "When you are stronger, we will walk in the gardens, until then…" he rose to his full height, the child craned her neck following him up, "…until then, rest," he said. He was about to turn on his heel and leave the room, but Beth reached up and took his massive hand, kissed the back of it and held it to her soft cheek, then letting it go, she lay back on her pillows and closed her eyes. Fuldus turned quickly to leave the room. He did not want Emma to see his glassy eyes and barely suppressed elation at an act of kindness so small that it could almost fell a giant such as him.

The Dream

The summer did end, as all do. The autumn was warm and a spectacle of reds and golden browns, but the winter, long and harsh, soon replaced any memory of it. Beth grew strong again and was to all intent and purpose her old self. Emma had questioned her many times about the events on the bridge, but Beth remembered very little, which Emma thought to be the best thing. Dreams disturbed the girl, though, which she could never remember.

Fuldus had visited them often and even brought gifts at the winter solstice. Emma was given a shawl woven from the finest angora. Beth was presented with a set of mirrors and a hairbrush, also a doll with a porcelain face and silk robes trimmed with lace. Fuldus said it came from a place very far away called the Orient.

Beth and Emma would make up stories of what the place was like. Emma said it was no doubt like any other. People worked and cooked and children would get up to no good, she would say with a wink.

Beth on the other hand said, if she closed her eyes and thought of the place 'really hard', she could see it. Strange buildings made of wood, painted red and gold. People worked in fields, up to their ankles in water. They carried paper umbrellas to keep the hot sun from their faces, and the children, she would say, were the most beautiful she had ever seen. She would describe things in such detail it would make Emma cry a little. Beth could never understand why.

Beth asked Emma why Fuldus never stayed long. Emma told the child that he had many things to attend to. "The country doesn't look after itself," she would say.

Fuldus did indeed have things to attend to. The invasion of the north had not happened as expected. The weather, his generals thought, had made the crossing too treacherous. His spies said nothing of any note that would explain why his troops sat in the northern snows of the cruellest winter for many decades. There had been reports of dissent amongst some of his men, and floggings had to be meted out to restore order. The hill tribes and men from the north were at least used to the weather, but those less accustomed to the icy winds and bone-gnawing cold were beginning to feel the effects of being away from southern home comforts.

The last intelligence reports listed one hundred and twenty-six dead, without a shot being fired nor an axe being thrown in anger. Supplies were being rationed, and the mood around the camps was becoming uneasy. There had been desertions and summary executions of those caught abandoning their posts. Local villagers had reported petty theft from farms, and one village was said to have been ransacked, being entirely looted of livestock and grain. The fleet was, at the time of the report being sent, trapped by sea ice. Hulls were being cracked as a result and the fear was when the thaw came most of the fleet would end up at the bottom of the sea. The sky ships were fairing no better. Engines were all but frozen and the last dozen scheduled patrols had not managed to get airborne.

Fuldus pushed the report across his desk in disgust. He looked to those assembled, but none could tell him with any authority if the Brotherhood's plans had changed. The intelligence gathered was still pointing to an invasion from the sea, and until that changed, his armies were best stationed around Elgin. Fuldus dismissed everyone and sat alone for hours in his war room like a brooding child waiting for a war it seemed would never come, as long as winter held sway over the islands.

Beth told Emma she understood why Fuldus never stayed long, but she did not really. The two of them would sit in the warmth of their rooms and watch the snowfall as if they had not a care in the world. The short days by the fire and the long quiet winter nights drinking soup came one after the other with nothing to disturb them but Beth's dreams, and that night was no different.

The morning sun was not yet up. Watery pinks and yellows were slowly colouring the sky to the east of the city when Emma, who was just re-lighting the fire, heard a voice behind her, "I had that dream again last night."

Emma turned, startled, dropping a small bundle of kindling. "My goodness, child, what are you doing up now?" She smiled and took a step towards Beth and smoothing her hair, she asked, "Is the bed ablaze?"

Beth returned the smile but had a distant air about her. "I was walking in a beautiful garden," she said. Emma fell silent and gave Beth all her attention, gently taking her hand as if to guide her in her story. "I can still smell flowers and hear birds," she paused as if troubled.

"Go on, Beth, what is it?" urged Emma.

Beth took a small gulp of air and continued, "I could hear, someone calling me, but it was more than that, it was as if the wind or the silence was calling, it was like I was being pulled." Emma interrupted, almost dismissive of the idea, her lips parted as if to speak, but Beth continued unaware. "I could feel warmth from the sun and the moon, there were stars and light, branches and then a clearing, and before I realised, I had my hand on a rough wooden door in a red brick wall. The wall was so high I could not see the top, the calling was almost unbearable." Beth was speaking hastily, and her voice had dropped to a whisper, eyes narrowed. Emma was becoming concerned. Beth, then looking down at her fingers, pulled a splinter from one, as a tear rolled down her cheek. "The door was hot," she said, becoming more animated. "It was hot when I touched it!" Still looking at her hands, she mumbled inaudibly and tried to stand, only to lurch forwards and fall to her knees and collapse in a sobbing heap.

Emma pulled the crying girl to her feet to comfort her, making soothing noises and placing a shawl around her shoulders. "Beth," she whispered, giving her a small shake. "Beth don't fret so. We will sort this out, now go and wash your face and brush your hair." Emma gave Beth the sweetest reassuring smile, "We will go and talk to someone about this and see if we can make some sense of it all." Beth looked up, her tear-streaked face a little calmer and offered up a thin smile. "That's more like it, girl," Emma chuckled, "Now, when the sun is fully up, we will go to the market and talk with Mother Dove-Coop."

Mother Dove-Coop sat and patiently listened to the girl, her gloved fingers nimbly plaiting strands of ribbon, which she sold at the winter markets along with corn dollies and candles. She could tell Beth was struggling to recall the dream. She raised her hand and Beth fell silent. "I find, sweetie, that the best way to re-tell a dream," she paused and took a sip from a cup of sweet nettle tea, "the best way to recall a dream is to re-enter it."

Emma looked concerned and spoke first. "Is that safe, Mother?" she enquired.

What, Mother Dove-Coop wondered, *could be so dangerous about returning to a beautiful garden?*

She reached by memory under the table at which she was seated and produced a small velvet bag and placed it before her. "Beth," she said softly, "you do trust me, don't you, sweetie?"

Beth nodded, then remembering Mother Dove-Coop's blindness, whispered, "Yes, of course."

"Good, good," said the old woman cheerily, "Now place your hands flat on the table in front of you and close your eyes." Beth duly obliged. "I want you," said Mother Dove-Coop, "to smell the perfume in the air and feel the breeze on your face." Birdsong began to fill the girl's head and she could feel the warmth of the sun and smell flowers once again. She was beginning to drift back to the garden.

Emma sat silently, watching intently. Mother Dove-Coop, still talking softly, reached inside the velvet bag and produced a small brass cup on a length of delicate chain and a tiny hammer. She held the two objects just above the table and striking one against the other, began to make barely audible chimes.

Beth, now in the garden, could hear the sound as if it were a distant church bell. Then on the breeze was a voice, comforting and reassuring. "Beth," it called. "Beth, my child, look down." Beth, completely at ease, did just that. "Feel the cold stones under your feet, follow the path." The voice urged, "Follow, follow."

The sky was clear, the sun was dropping, and the full moon was beginning to rise above the trees. Beth walked on through a tangle of branches and into the clearing she had found herself in the night before. There, just as then, was the red brick wall and the rough wooden door. She could not help but feel uneasy; part of her wanted to see what was on the other side, yet equally afraid, she stayed rooted to the spot. The branches of the trees rustled, the voice in the breeze was calling. "Beth," it sighed, "the door, go to the door."

Unaware of moving, Beth found herself with her hand pressed flat against the rough wood. She was suddenly overcome with a sense of euphoria, the sky above burst to life, stars danced, and supernovas exploded like fireworks, the door began to vibrate and become warm, and then hot. The heat was causing splinters to smoulder, wisps of smoke began to rise from it. Tears of joy were in her eyes. She felt all the questions she had ever, were about to be answered. The door was glowing white hot now. The heat from it made her hands and her arms up to her shoulders glow, but she felt no pain. The door was beginning to crumble, white hot dust filling the air and falling in smouldering chunks to the floor.

"Beth," the whispers were back in her head now, "see the door, see the door," they urged.

The distant church bells continued to chime. Beth looked once more to the door, there it stood but just as solid and rough as it was before. "Open your hand, open your hand."

Beth gazed down at her tightly clenched fist and watched as it unfurled to reveal a heavy wrought iron key. This time, the voice was more urgent and insistent. "Take the key child and place it in the lock."

The key fitted perfectly. Beth was giddy. What was on the other side? She was desperate to know. "Calm yourself, breathe deeply."

The voices, and the chimes were now indistinguishable from each other. Beth could feel herself slipping away, losing control, her hand still on the key, fear beginning to take hold.

"Yes," chimed the voice, "you are safe in the garden." Beth was beginning to agree. "Yes," she said softly, "safe in the garden, good child," hummed the voice, "Now, turn the key," Beth did as she was instructed, pausing waiting for the door to open. "The door is locked, you have locked the door," chimed the soft voice. "Now go," it insisted, "and think of it no more."

Beth opened her eyes. She was in bed. "How? Wasn't I...?" She jumped from the warm sheets.

Emma turned to her with a welcoming grin. "Goodness, girl, you fair gave me a turn, but I'll dare say nothing gets you out of bed like the smell of bacon frying." Before Beth could say anything else, a soft kiss was planted on her forehead, "Now, wash the sleep from your eyes and sit down, breakfast will be ready in just a minute." Emma turned back to the spitting iron pan and Beth washed her face. They both ate breakfast before going about their day.

The Letter

The mud was almost impossible to negotiate. The thaw, when it came, came swiftly. Men, horses and waggons alike became mired and immobile. After the victory, engineers involved in the ground assault made gantry walkways so the officers could move around more freely.

Two officers approached the field of battle. A battle only recently finished. The older of the two men spoke first. "Surprise," he said. "Surprise is the best weapon of all."

The younger man nodded his agreement. He coughed as he surveyed the twisted, charred wreckage that lay all around him and as far as the eye could see. Bodies half submerged in water and blood, hands and faces contorted, the final moments of dying men recorded in earth. The air was still alive with ash and soot and the smell of a thousand fires.

The planks were laid between what had been, until recently, rows of tents now reduced to squares of blackened rags and poles, pointing accusingly to the leaden sky from where fire had rained. Bodies still lying in cots, caught unaware by the swiftness of the attack. *The planks, if laid end to end,* thought the younger man, *would have stretched for a thousand miles.*

He stepped from the walkway into what was, merely hours ago, a billet for a dozen men, judging by the number of cots still standing. He prodded about with the toes of his boots, disturbing the ashes, the remnants of a book, water bottles and other items one would expect in such a place.

Following the paths through the battlefield brought the two men to the foot of a small hill, which ten minutes later they were atop. The ground was scorched like the rest. The hill gave an uninterrupted view of the northern sea to the east.

The churning black waters now busy with the arrival of Dragon-headed warships. Swaggering into harbour like pleasure boats returning from a regatta, their colours brazenly flying and steam whistles screaming their arrival.

The lookout post which they had climbed to was probably the furthest point from the start of the attack. The body of a man, probably a sentry lay amongst its ruins. Taken by surprise just as the rest were, he would have witnessed the full horror of the attack before he was cut down. It seemed he had made no attempt to escape. They were about to head back down the hill when the younger man's foot inadvertently struck a small tin box partly submerged in ash. He stooped to pick it up, and instinctively shook it. Its contents made dull thuds like the ringing of a muffled bell. The box appeared plain; if it had sported any kind of design, it would have been seared from its surface. It's intricacies and subtleties lost to the fires.

The box was roughly six-inches square, three-inches deep and still warm to the touch. Once prised open, the contents of the box appeared unremarkable: a penknife, a set of gaming dice and a wad of folded papers, baked yellow and crisped by the heat. He closed the box and pushed it into his pocket.

The two men found themselves once again amongst their own troops. Their main task currently was damping down stubborn hot-spots and disposing of the dead. Trenches had been dug, and into which bodies, without any ceremony or reverence, were being hurled and hurriedly covered over. The men returned to their respective quarters to freshen up before dinner. The younger man had found no joy in the victory of the day, he could taste ash and wondered what else he was ingesting. He slumped back onto his rickety cot, then making himself as comfortable as possible took the tin box from his pocket. He removed the papers and carefully folded them back, so they lay flat. The outer pages cracked as they separated.

There was an IOU for tobacco and ale, a debt which would now go unpaid. There were some surprisingly good sketches of the surrounding landscape, and a letter. He settled back and read:

"Waterside Farm
Gillingham
Kent

My Dearest,
It feels like I have been gone from you longer than I have known you. I am sitting here looking south, wishing I was by your side. What I would not give for our warm bed, and a homecooked meal. Yes, I know I always joke about your cooking, but that is how much I miss you. How's our little Caleb, not so little I am guessing? How are you and Pa coping with the farm? Up here, most of the local's livestock was confiscated to feed the troops. I hope we did not suffer the same fate down there.
There is talk of some of us being stood down, whoever was supposed to invade seems to have lost all interest in such an enterprise, maybe they care even less for our weather than us. I pray I am home for the spring planting and we could make an early start on repairs to the cottage walls and thatch. Have I missed the little one starting to walk? Tell him about me, so when I come home, I am not a stranger to him. Are his eyes still as blue as yours?
When I come home, we could think about a brother or a sister for him. I know I said we should wait, but now I regret it. I have come to think we should have at least twelve children. They can run the farm while we drink cider under the apple tree in the garden. Do you remember Gillan, that big fella who did some reaping for us a couple of seasons ago? Red-headed, hands like shovels. Well, he is in the same billet as me. I always thought he was a lazy beggar, but it was good to see a familiar face, then it made me think of the farm and you again.
I swear if they don't send me home soon, I will start walking. Keep the kettle on the fire, not for tea. I will want to soak my blisters while I am drinking some good ale. Then we

can dance and sing and pretend I have just come in from the fields after an honest days' work. I was never cut out for soldiering, and if I see another musket or short sword again, it will be a day too soon. So, kiss our boy for me and think of me every now and then. I will be home before you both know it.

Until then, my love x"

He folded the pages back on themselves and momentarily thought of home, his mother and sisters. He sat up and reached into his satchel and pulled out a sheet of writing paper and a pen. At the top of the paper, he wrote,

"Waterside Farm, Gillingham, Kent." He thought for a few moments before continuing, *"Madam, it is with regret I have to inform you of the death of your husband. Please know that he spoke of you fondly before he passed. He fought bravely but succumbed to his injuries in the field. I have enclosed at his request the last letter he wrote you and your son."*

He folded his note into an envelope and placed the charred letter with it, then stepping out into the darkening night, he called for a clerk. "See to it this is delivered," he said and with that returned to his tent to dress for dinner.

While shaving, he asked his reflection: Would his superiors understand this simple act of kindness? *Probably not,* he told himself, and thought no more of it.

Later that night in the officers' mess, the mood was subdued. The younger man was joined by his companion from earlier in the day. They ate a meal of bread, cheese and ham. They drank a particularly sour red wine. He enquired of the younger man, "Is it as you remember it?"

He dabbed the corners of his mouth with a crisp white napkin. "No," he said, "I never made it this far north, before I was..." he paused and considered his next words carefully, "...sent home."

"You were lucky," said the older man, "How did that happen?"

"I was a very sickly child, I had stowed away on my father's ship because I wasn't well enough to travel with him during the original campaign; it was the one time in my life that looking half my age seemed like a virtue," he said with a wry smile. "Had I been a strapping fourteen-year-old, I more than likely would have suffered the same fate as my father."

The older man nodded in understanding. "Well," he said, "you are undoubtedly the only one amongst us to have met that barbarian and lived to tell your remarkable story."

The younger man finished his glass of wine with a grimace, then standing, he took his leave. His companion gave him an understanding smile and told him with a polite nod to sleep well. "Tomorrow, we head south," he added as the youngster disappeared from sight, then raising his voice shouted, "Good night, Kristan."

The Return

The citadel was uncommonly quiet, thought Mrs Cooper. She placed the warm eggs she had collected into the basket she was carrying and closed the hen house door. The sounds of the market outside the citadel walls were drifting across the courtyard as normal, and the kitchen was playing its usual tune of chiming pots and pans preparing breakfast for the garrison, but that wasn't it. She could not put her finger on it. It was just uncommonly quiet.

Back in the kitchen, the scullery girls and the porters were readying trollies laden with hot bread, porridge, bacon and implausibly large steaming pots of sweet tea. The clock struck its single chime on the half hour; thirty minutes more and the mess hall would see the six o'clock stampede of hungry guards.

The wagon-train of trollies set off across the courtyard cobbles for its three-minute voyage. Then duly unloaded, they made a more serene return. Molly, a relative newcomer to the kitchen staff, stood as she had for the last six months, waiting to feed the scowling, bleary-eyed hoard. She knew none of their names and as far as she knew, they didn't know hers either.

The clock in the hall struck six, she glanced towards the double-panelled doors and waited for them to be barged off their hinges. She waited and waited. She became transfixed on the doors. Five past, ten past, a quarter after.

Mrs Cooper couldn't believe her eyes when Molly walked back into the kitchen. "Not one of them," she said incredulously, "not one of them has come in for breakfast." She wiped flour from her hands and tossed aside the tea towel she had used. She found herself in the courtyard once more.

"Jasper," she called, "Jasper Thompson!" She turned full circle looking all around her. Nobody responded, not a soul. "Hello!" she called again, still nothing. She was becoming more concerned as the minutes passed and found herself drifting towards the barracks' door.

She grasped its cold iron handle. "Hello," she said once more, and then pushed her way into the room which was dark and silent. She squinted as her eyes adjusted to the gloom. Shafts of light sliced through the gaps in the drapes, glowing chalk lines burning on the floor and walls. "Hello," her voice was starting to quake a little. She was expecting snoring and then dozens of embarrassed giants to leap from their bunks, stumbling over one another as they realised the consequences of having overslept, but all there was, was silence.

Molly stood in the kitchen looking across the square, now obsessed with the barracks' doors, waiting for Mrs Cooper to re-emerge. Her eyes were beginning to ache, as she continued her unblinking staring. She almost didn't react when Mrs Cooper stumbled back into view; she could see her mouth moving but no sound, no words. She watched as she dropped to her knees, and still did not react. It was not until the most anguished sound she had ever heard rent the air that she reacted. She found herself dashing across the courtyard, barely able to stay upright; she was moving so swiftly.

Mrs Cooper was sobbing. Molly was trying to understand her whimpers and wails. Finally, their eyes met, Mrs Copper swallowed hard. She mouthed a word, then managed to form it properly and release it to the air. "Dead," she whispered. "They are all dead."

Fuldus was awake now. His guards had entered his room and informed him of a disturbance in the courtyard. They knew the drill; at any sign of trouble, they would form a cordon around his chambers. He was hastily informed of the details. Poisoned, he was informed. The men, soldiers, the battle hounds, sentries, armourers—all dead.

His generals and advisers were not exempt, all those not in the field had suffered the same fate. Anyone, in fact, who could hold a sword was dead or missing. To all intents and purposes, Fuldus and the citadel were unprotected.

The main door from the corridor opened and to his relief, Emma entered, dragging a bemused Beth behind her. They were ushered to the furthest of his rooms. They would be safest there, a corner suite looking over the market and out along the river, sheer on two sides. The only way to attack was from the corridor through which they had just entered.

When Fuldus joined them, Emma was sitting, cradling Beth, reassuring her as best as she could. He was safe in the knowledge he could not be harmed, but they would still need protecting. Three hundred hand-picked warriors were gone. Only the two dozen or so with him now stood between whoever had poisoned the citadel guards and all else he held dear.

The next few hours passed with a leaden fluidity. Fuldus would wander back and forth from room to room, conferring with the few who were still alive. A messenger had been dispatched to the nearest garrison to ascertain their situation, but nothing had been heard. The kitchen, and other staff, had been ordered to continue as if nothing had happened and lunch was to be prepared.

The sun now stood at its highest vantage point, bathing the market below in early spring sunshine. Trade continued unaffected by the events within the citadel walls. Mothers bought cloth, yarn for mending, and food for dinner. Buskers sang songs while the perpetual haggling continued as it did every day the market was on the bridge. The world outside went about its business, not knowing, and to all intents and purposes, not caring.

Then, at the far end of the market a sudden commotion; a rider had entered the bridge and was galloping through the stalls, scattering the crowds as he ploughed his way towards the citadel. Fuldus rushed to the balcony and leaned to get a closer look at who was steering the steed with such skill. Shouts of general abuse were being hurled at the onrushing man. As he came closer, and without allowing the horse time to fully come to a halt, the rider, dressed from head to foot in white, dismounted in such a dramatic fashion that those who were only a few moments prior abusing him could not help but find themselves impressed.

The rider took a deep breath and stood as straight as he could, proud and gleaming. Bathing in the sun's warmth he cut an imposing figure. Those in the market had begun to crowd around him, eager to see why he was there. He looked up, cleared his throat and yelled, "False King!"

From the height of his balcony, Fuldus could not make out the man's face, but he could see he was pointing, arm outstretched to his left and off into the distance. Fuldus slowly craned his head in the direction the stranger was indicating. The sun glinting on the water made it difficult to focus, but in the distance, he could make out a dozen or more ships making their way along the Thames towards the citadel. Behind them like a mist on the horizon were more ships than he could count; however, at the head of the column was a grand, white steamship, its paddle wheels pounding the water, the only ship he recognised, and it was approaching with impatient speed.

Smaller fishing boats were doing their best to avoid being sunk by the rapidly advancing armada. Some were capsized in the wake as they sped past. The figure in white had remounted his horse and was gesturing to the crowd. There were signs of confusion and panic accompanied by a considerable increase in crowd noise. General murmurs became screams and barked panicked calls to evacuate the market.

As the stampede began, the white ship boomed, sending a cannonball crashing into the water not fifty feet from the market stalls. Whether this was a warning shot, or its gunner had just fallen short of his target, no one cared; the occupants of the market and the buildings on the bridge were disappearing at incredible speeds. Another boom sent water showering onto the cobble-stoned road.

The rider in white had positioned himself as close to the citadel gates as humanly possible to take shelter. The advancing ship fired again, this time the bridge was struck with full force. The wall and part of the road crumbled to dust and fell away into the river. Taking their cue from the direct hit, the other gunners began firing. The bridge was being struck repeatedly. As the market burned, buildings tumbled apart, glass shattered, and timbers snapped. Chimney stacks became a sum of their parts, red bricks spiralling into the air and bombarding the cobbles below. A smoke screen was rising, briefly shrouding the bridge from Fuldus' view. He turned to his remaining guards and ordered them to the hallway outside his chamber. They drew their swords and duly obliged.

Fuldus returned to the window, the dust and smoke had cleared somewhat, he could now see the extent to which the bridge had been damaged. He was as isolated from his armies, he thought, as the citadel was now isolated from Fulham. The bridge was all but destroyed. A yawning chasm some hundreds of yards wide let the glistening river below sparkle through. The sound of churning water and the hiss of steam engines were now unavoidable. Beth sat with her hands cupping her ears. Emma had picked her up and moved as far away from the door as possible, but the child, still, was visibly distressed.

Voices could now be heard from the ships, calls for, "Engines stop!" and orders for ropes to be secured. There was a sound of grinding and screeching as the hull of the white ship scrapped the jagged edges of the bridge and ground to a halt at the newly formed jetty in front of the citadel.

The ship halted, creating a wall between the city and the entrance to the citadel. There was a moment of silence, and then a deafening clang as gleaming metal gangplanks smashed down onto the broken cobbles on both sides of the bridge, forming a highway between the citadel and what remained of the market.

Dozens of white-uniformed soldiers streamed from the ship. A cannon was swiftly assembled and took aim at the doors, reducing them to splinters. The citadel was breached and undefended, columns of soldiers walked unopposed into the square and began to secure the area, rounding up those who appeared to pose a threat and confining the rest to the kitchens.

The screams of fighting outside of his rooms brought Fuldus' attention back to his immediate predicament. He must find a way for him and Beth to escape. The hallway was out of the question, and he had no rope to drop from the window. Trapped, he had no option but to fight his way to freedom. "Beth," he said as calmly as possible, "stay behind me." But before he could take another step, the door was flung open and six pike-wielding soldiers barred his way.

He drew the short sword from his belt and inhaled deeply. "Are we feeling brave today, gentleman?" he said to those standing before him as he adopted a stance to repel their attack. None answered nor moved, but before he could say another word, a disembodied voice drifted from the hallway.

"Fuldus, my old friend, I have so looked forward to this moment."

The soldiers parted, not taking their eyes from Fuldus, as the white-robed Keeper of the Secrets entered the room with the ease of one who had been invited, and directly behind him was his pocket-sized companion, the Keeper of the Laws, as usual, clad in red.

Fuldus stepped back. He could still barely contain his hatred of the man, and the passage of time had not diminished it. The mere sight of them in their robes made his head swim, he felt nauseated and his ears rang.

The old man in white walked across the room and sat at the large desk, much to Fuldus' obvious annoyance. He made himself comfortable and gave him a thin smile before saying, "We have much to discuss." He clasped his hands in front of him. "Much to discuss," he repeated, "our adventures, as much fun as they have been, are at an end, so I must be brief."

He leaned to one side as if to look past Fuldus and at those standing behind him. "You, woman," he said softly. Emma made eye contact with him but did not move. "You have nothing to fear from me, step forward." Fuldus had no time to say anything before Emma brushed past him and approached, dropping to her knees in front of the man, as if to beg for mercy.

He stood and reached out a hand. "Oh, Sister Forthright, please rise," he said, "It is time to return to your sisters." Fuldus was clearly confused by what was unfolding, the Keeper carried on regardless, as if he and the woman were alone in the room. "Your work these past years has been exemplary."

The woman was now standing, and openly weeping, she leaned and grasped the Keeper's hand, kissing it fervently. "Bless you, my lord," she whispered, "I have been counting the days until your return, I cannot tell how great my joy…"

The old man raised his other hand and she fell silent. "Leave us now and re-join the good sisters at Gallows Hill."

She released him, and after brushing the creases from her smock, spun on her heel to glare at Fuldus. Clearing her throat, she sneered and spat in his face, then left the room as instructed.

The Keeper once again turned his attention to Fuldus. "I sense your confusion, so allow me to enlighten you." He cleared his throat, "Miss Forthright," he indicated in the direction of the door and the disappearing woman, "Emma as you knew her, has been working," he paused, "covertly through all these years, a dedicated sister of the cause," the Keeper of the Secrets was revelling in his title as he continued his explanation, "as was one Mister Jasper Thompson, who at great risk to himself last night, entertained your guard with frivolous songs and witty stories whilst poisoning all the water, ale and food in the barrack house and kennels, leaving your citadel as quiet as a nursery after bedtime."

He was growing weary and seated himself once more. "Also, as well as the valiant Mister Thompson, there was, of course, Mister Toliver." He gave a self-satisfied smile, "I sent you an inept assassin, in return you sent me your armies."

Fuldus' eyes narrowed, the elaborate nature of the deception dawning on him. The Keeper of the Secrets intended to enjoy this moment for as long as he could safely do so. "Yes, Fuldus," he continued, "Mr Toliver came to you full to the brim with choice information, but it was information I wanted you to have. Your army marched north at my whim, then it sat through the worst winter in decades to be caught bogged down in mud by my own air fleet and consumed in minutes by a storm of fire." Fuldus was shaken by the news of the fate of his troops and with mocking sympathy, the Keeper added, "I'm afraid dead men don't march south very quickly, my friend, it would appear you are quite alone."

The Keeper, emboldened by the sight of Fuldus reeling and helpless, raised his voice "Now!" he said, "We had an agreement, you and I."

Fuldus was genuinely taken aback. "What agreement?" he snorted.

The bejewelled smile widened and asked, "Do you know, Fuldus, why Oracles and their kind are called the Children of Summer?"

Fuldus was becoming irritated. "What agreement?" he barked.

With that, and not to press his luck, the Keeper of Secrets waved his hand. The soldiers in the doorway moved aside, a shadow crept across the floor as a chained woman shuffled into the room. Fuldus let out an audible gasp. *Impossible,* he thought, this was the woman he had released from the Chapel. The architect of his plans. His protector, the answer to his question. She was identical in every way, her dress, her demeanour, the gloom she brought with her, even the sadness in her eyes, but that woman was gone. How was she now here?

"Oracles," said the old man, "born under the sign of Gemini, the summer sign." Fuldus was struggling to see the relevance of this lesson in lore. "Oracles," the Keeper continued, "the useful commodity that they are, are always born as..." The man's eyes narrowed, as if he was waiting for a schoolboy to eagerly shout an answer, but when no answer was forthcoming, he finished his sentence, "...born as twins."

The Keeper was now in full swing, finding his explanations and their effect enormously satisfying. "One injured and left for you," pausing, purely for dramatic effect, "to liberate but with very clear instructions as to what to offer." The woman in chains was visibly aging with the passing seconds, clearly pained by the role she had played in events. The old man laughed, "And this one, a bargaining chip, with a world of pain and suffering available to her should her sister not comply with those instructions."

Fuldus could see now, the cruel harshness of the past winter that had taken such a toll on his troops was not mere chance, it had been waited upon to serve a purpose. The Keeper was clearly not restricted to one question of his Oracle but free to draw from her well of knowledge whenever it suited him. Fuldus stood coiled like a spring, ready to make for the door as soon as an opportunity presented itself. He would just let the old man talk until it did.

"But I digress, let me get back to our agreement," he said. "You were promised a reign eternal. Allowing you to secure the homeland, whilst I made allies of our common enemies and expanded our empire." Laughing aloud now, he went on, "the Scandinavians hate you almost as much as I do," a pause and then he regained his train of thought. "Our agreement!" he said with renewed vigour. "Preposterous as it was, we needed you to take the bait. We had to offer you a prize so beguiling, even a man of the greatest moral fibre would find it impossible to resist." He took a swig of water from a glass that was standing on the desk, he swallowed and grimaced. "Urgh, stale," he said. "You saw eternity placed within your grasp and grabbed it with both greedy hands."

"The Brotherhood knew of your plans to overthrow us, but before I could move against you, the Scandinavians took us both by surprise," he coughed out a small laugh, "that's the problem with Oracles," he said, "they do not offer warnings freely."

"So," he went on, "you and your rabble saved us, and that left you like a mighty oak, we could not topple you, we had to let you rot from the inside, become weak," he paused, "and now we are here, all we need to do is give you the gentlest of pushes to bring you crashing down." The Keeper glanced around the room, "The Oracle you discovered," he jerked a wrinkled finger in the direction of the woman in chains, "this one's twin, offered you what I wanted you to have, and to a degree, you have had it, but now it's time for the agreement to be dissolved."

Fuldus could hear the conversation he had all those years ago in his head as clearly as if it were just yesterday. "Until you choose to end your life, you will rule, and no one can end it for you." He smiled, safe in the knowledge he had no intention of ending his life, or consequently his reign.

Fuldus smiled. "Well," he said, "if you are as well informed as you say you are, you will know..."

But before he could finish, the smaller man in the red robes produced a small bell and struck it sharply once. Fuldus took a step towards him as the Keeper of the Secrets raised his hand, "Now, Fuldus, do not act in haste, or you will have an eternity in which to repent." Fuldus turned back to the old man who was still speaking. "I am, as you yourself said, very well informed. I know what you were told, I know your grasp on power ends when you choose to end your own life, I know all this." The old man paused to catch his breath, and as he did, he opened a small pouch which, until now, had hung unnoticed from his wrist.

He slowly leaned towards Fuldus with his arm outstretched. "Here," he said, "this is for you." Fuldus looked at the man's hand. Between his thumb and index finger, he was holding a small, red, glass bottle, beautifully ornate with a tiny cork as a stopper.

Fuldus snorted. "And what exactly is that?" he asked.

"Poison," replied the Keeper in a very matter-a-fact fashion.

"Poison," repeated Fuldus, who then threw his head back and roared with laughter. "You expect me to poison myself?" he bellowed.

The Keeper was stony faced. "Yes," he said passively, "yes, I do, and yes, you will." With that, he jerked his head in the direction of the window, Fuldus turned slightly to see what he was looking at. He squinted as his eyes adjusted to the sunlight. With no understanding of why, there standing, swaying on the window ledge, was Beth.

The breeze was rippling her dark hair and billowing her simple dress. Fuldus was about to dart across the room and pull her to him for safe keeping, but before he could move, the bell held aloft by the Keeper of the Laws chimed once more, and Beth took a tiny step closer to the edge. Fuldus turned and glared at the man with the bell dangling between his red-painted fingernails. He took a few lunging steps in his direction when the Keeper of the Secrets urged him to stop. "Think carefully before you take another step." Fuldus, grinding his teeth and fists clenched, halted in mid stride. "Control yourself, this will all be over soon, my friend," he said soothingly. Taking his place standing by his companion, the Keeper of the Secrets continued, "Fuldus," he said, "I know you will not allow the child to come to any harm."

As much as Fuldus knew this to be the case, he did not wish the man before him to see the extent to which it was true. "Fuldus, I never had you pegged as a sentimental being," said the Keeper of the Secrets. "You had one tiny advantage, and that was the question you could ask your Oracle." Fuldus kept glancing over his shoulder to Beth, she seemed completely unaware of her predicament. The Keeper continued, "One question, any knowledge or information was yours to demand, but what did you do?" A mocking tone now entered his voice, "Will the child live?" he sarcastically sobbed. Fuldus looked back to the man talking, the pain of that day once again etched on his face, "Yes!" said the Keeper of the Secrets, "There it is! The reason you will not leave this room alive." He clasped his hands together with glee. "The last bargain we shall make Fuldus, the child's life for yours."

Fuldus was at the point of exploding with rage, but he finally realised how precarious the situation was. Still the talking persisted. "You see, my friend, my inept assassin's tiny bullet was never meant for you." Glancing to the window, with his bejewelled smile in full view, he said, "It was always meant for the girl, a device to make her even more precious to you than your poor departed sister, your dead mother."

Fuldus' head was spinning, he could feel the invisible pull to protect Beth, but he dared not move, the silent chimes still ringing in his head. The old man secure in the knowledge his victory was imminent, forged onwards with his speech. "Rather than ask a question that would further your plans, you asked after the one thing more important to you than all else— her!" He pointed at Beth. "And now you will give up your life to do the one thing you could not do for your mother, your sister." Fuldus was weak at the knees, all his past failures distilled into one critical moment. "I see your pain my friend," said the Keeper with what sounded like genuine concern, "but this situation does not have to end in tragedy, you can still save this child."

Fuldus breathed slowly for a few moments, forcing himself to calm. He stared at the man before him. "What if I choose not to play your game?" he growled.

The old man put his gnarled fist to his lips to control a small cough. "Then, I'm sorry, there will be consequences," he said. "Just so you understand," he continued, "the bell and its chimes have been yours and the girl's constant companion. Its whispering, guiding you to this place, this time and these events." The old man was beginning to look as haggard as the chained Oracle, and thus an urgency entered his voice. "So, one more chime and the girl steps from the window." Fuldus turned back to Beth. "If you make a move towards me, the bell will chime, and the girl steps from the window. If you strike my companion, the bell will chime and the girl; I am sure I do not need repeat myself again."

The old man sat back in the chair, "Any action other than the one I want or is ordained will end badly for you both. The girl will be dead on the cobbles, and you will end your days with an eternity to regret your final failure, and I think, as we have already established, that is not want you want."

The bottle was raised and offered to him once more. "I hope my clarification of the situation has helped you come to the correct conclusion, your voluntary end is her only salvation," said The Keeper of the Secrets with an air of finality. "Drink it and she lives; anything else and she dies."

It felt like an eternity had passed, "Time," said Fuldus to himself as much as to anyone else.

"No!" barked the Keeper of the Secrets, "You have no more time. Drink or the girl dies!"

Fuldus found his eyes drawn to the Oracle. Her appearance was changing, a warm glow had returned to her face, she looked younger now and a smile was forming on her lips. "And why are you suddenly so happy?" he asked.

There was a gentleness in her response that took him by surprise, "I have seen the death of you," she sighed.

Fuldus snorted. "And that makes you smile."

"Yes, it does, my love," she replied.

The blood in Fuldus, boiling moments before, calmed, serenity returned to him; he knew the course he must take. He could see the trembling fingers holding the bell, the sweat forming on the small man's brow. *The bell will always chime,* he thought to himself. What chances for his Little Death if he did as they asked? What would become of her then? Would she be cared for, protected as he had tried to protect her, loved, he could admit it to himself now at least, loved as he loved her?

"You are right old man," Fuldus said with resolve, "I failed my mother and sister." He looked to the Oracle and smiled, "but I will not fail her."

He reached out and carefully picked up the small red bottle. He peered at it, tiny, glinting menacingly in his giant palm, his thumb and index finger barely able to remove the cork, his eyes met the Keeper of the Secrets as he hurled the bottle and its contents at his tormentor. The old man shrieked as the vial whizzed past him. Fuldus glanced over his shoulder and, before anyone could react, had turned and launched himself across the room, grabbing Beth as he did and the two of them tumbled out of the open window.

Together they plummeted towards the cobblestones below. Fuldus rolled his body in mid-air so he was looking towards the sun. He straightened his arms and held Beth as far from him as he could, certain in the knowledge that he would hit the ground first and she, surviving the impact would at least have a chance at escape. He closed his eyes and braced himself.

When the impact came, it was not as he imagined. There was no pain, the ground seemed to have softened and cushioned their landing. He was still holding Beth aloft. Opening one eye, he could see the blue sky above them. Turning on his side, he laid Beth in the tall grass, which moments before had not been there. Where were the cobbles and shattered red bricks, the ship, the river, the city?

Beth sat upright and yawned as if waking from an afternoon nap, stretching her arms wide as she did. Fuldus was sitting now, running his hands through the lush green grass. He inhaled the spring flower-scented air and smiled. Reason, though, came quickly to him. "Where are we?" he asked.

Beth, who had now wondered a few feet from him, turned and said, "We are in the garden, with trees that are one thousand feet tall." She laughed, and with that, giant cedars rocketed from the earth rushing skyward. A forest, ancient and stately, stood all around them. Fuldus was awed, terrified and giddy as a child all at the same time. Before he could ask another question, the cedars began to shrink and change, becoming oak, ash and sycamore in heavy autumn foliage. The air was alive with falling leaves, and a slight chill had replaced the warmth.

Fuldus looked down, Beth was holding his hand. She gazed up and smiled. The golden crisp leaves began to turn to dust, and the dust to delicate snowflakes. The forest was now sparkling with the beauty of a million diamonds. Fuldus dropped to his knees and looked deep into her eyes and asked gently, "Where are we?"

"You are wherever you want to be," she replied. "The garden, a forest, home."

Fuldus looked to the horizon, the sun was setting now, but in the distance, he could see the outlines of people walking towards them. He could not make out their faces, but he knew, he knew every last one of them. Tears began to roll down his cheeks. "Oh gods," he whispered, "the things I have done."

Beth's voice was fading but her words calmed him. "This is the price you must pay," she whispered. "You are feeling the pain you have inflicted on others, the minor slights to the horrors." Fuldus was weeping now. "By those here, you are already forgiven, and in time, you will learn to forgive others, and yourself," she said. He swallowed hard and stood tall, taking a step towards them, but he stopped, Beth was not moving.

He turned to her. "You must come too," he said. "Don't worry about me," she replied sweetly. "I will join you soon." She was dissolving into the darkening night, the warmth of her hand left his, but he could still hear her voice, "When I am here, I see things so clearly, but there," pausing, she said, "I think I have some things yet to do." Fuldus found himself alone in the snow, a full moon by some magical feat of alchemy had turned it golden. He took a tentative step towards the horizon. Overcome by fear he halted. Little Death's voice returned to him, "There is nothing here but love, all the love you denied yourself, be brave one last time, go to them." Her voice was gone, but on the wind, he was sure he heard her say, "Thank you, goodbye."

When the impact came, the sound was awful, his body crashing onto the unyielding stones, air and blood exploding from his lungs. Beth was flung to the ground, rolling for several yards. She sprang to her feet, dazed but unharmed. Her head was spinning, how was she outside now? Where was Emma? Where was Fuldus?

She turned from side to side, head still swimming. Trying to hear, trying to see. Her senses finally cooperating, there he was, he was outside too. She smiled fleetingly, then noticed the sticky red mass at her feet, filling the cracks in the cobblestones. Momentarily repulsed she leapt clear of the puddle forming around her. A dark footprint mimicked where she had landed. Her eyes followed the black lines from the puddle to what was causing it.

"No, no, no," was all she could manage to say. All the lines radiated from Fuldus. Stumbling to him, she dropped to her knees beside his still body. She had only ever seen him this quiet once before, the morning she spoke and he was in his giant bed, but this was not the same. His eyes were covered with a tangle of hair and blood. Her trembling hands gently wiped his face.

His eyes were closed, and there was no smile on his lips. "Fuldus," she whispered. "Fuldus," this time with more urgency. He had not moved or tried to brush her away as he had that morning. "Fuldus!" she sobbed while pounding on his chest. Her whole body convulsed, tiny fists pummelling him, knowing her efforts to wake him were pointless.

A mixture of grief and rage were beginning to swallow her. She could feel quicksand grabbing her ankles. Invisible tentacles pulling her under, sand filling her lungs. She was being pulled from him and she had no desire to go, he would be alone so she must stay.

Be brave, she said to herself, *be brave, one last time.* But imagine as she might she was in a quiet room; a storm was raging outside making the windows rattle and the shutters slam. She could not keep the wind at bay. No sooner would she bar one window, another would be thrown open and her torment would crash back in tearing the calm of the room asunder. It was too much for her tiny human heart to bear, and throwing her head back, she howled in anguish.

From above, the Keeper of the Secrets was yelling at the soldiers below to stop the girl from escaping. He turned to those in the room with him. "Get the girl! Get the girl!" he screamed. The room emptied in an instant. "How did this happen?" screeched the old man at the Oracle, but before she could answer, he had returned to the window.

Beth laid still clinging to Fuldus wishing to be as dead as him. But she had become aware of the screams and shouts around her. Forcing herself to sit up, she took one last look at his face and gently kissed his cheek. Then placing her hands on his chest, she said, "They will not have your body," and not knowing how, watched as her hands began to glow and shimmer, a heat haze grew around her *and* her fallen giant. "From the earth to the sky," she whispered. Onrushing soldiers halted their advance as the heat around her became impossible to approach. Fuldus' body was smouldering and slowly crumbling away, and when Beth stood, she was alone.

The haze that had engulfed them both cleared, no one dared to move. "The girl, take her now!" a shrill distant command ordered. One of the guards with a loaded crossbow, shaken by what he had seen and startled by the screaming from the window above, inadvertently loosed a bolt in Beth's direction. Three others followed suit thinking the order to kill had been given. The bolts streaked towards their intended target, but the instant they struck, they became ash and left nothing more than smudges on the child's dress. Battle hardened men were now retreating, even if it meant the gallows; they had no intention of attacking something that could incinerate bodies and destroy the cruellest oak arrows.

One of the Brotherhood, less perturbed by what he had seen, lunged forwards with his pike. The girl merely grasped the tip and fixed him with a stare that brought him to his knees, whilst his spear glowed white and disintegrated in his hands. The soldiers sent by the Keeper of the Secrets had now surrounded her, and forming a circle, they slowly advanced.

Beth did not want to harm anyone, but neither did she wish to be in the custody of the approaching men. She turned on the spot and counted sixteen guards. Exhausted and broken, she slumped to her knees, and closing her eyes, waited for their rough grasp.

The captain of the troop stepped forward, he reached towards the girl but halted, his expression of determination replaced by one of shock and confusion. The pike in his hands slipped from his grasp and fell with a clatter. He raised his right hand to his cheek. His fingers, as if they were tiny legs, walked the line of his jawbone to the back of his skull. He could feel no pain, but there, where his fingers came to rest, was a hard object, which was clearly not there moments earlier. He dropped to his knees and crashed face first to the ground.

Those with him could now see a small bone-handled knife which it was fair to assume had felled their companion. Then a whistling and a fizzing, as a smoking canister lobbed unseen, bounced to the cobbles, enveloping all in an acrid yellow smog. Coughing and spewing, the men searched in vain for a sight of their attacker. Another knife whizzed through the air, then another and another. The guards were in a half-blind retreat screaming and clawing at their faces and necks as they went.

Beth had not moved as the soldiers fell around her, but now she was finding it hard to breathe. Staggering to her feet, she could just make out the shape of a tall thin man striding towards her. His face was covered with a scarf, she had no idea who he was. His hands were working feverishly, one was clenched in a fist holding the many small knives which were proving so deadly, the other was dealing the blades like a gambler nonchalantly dealing cards.

The cries of the guards fell silent. The tall man, his hands now empty, reached down and grabbed Beth. He threw her over his shoulder like a bag of coal and began to make his way off the bridge. They were on the ship's gangplank before any more soldiers tried to impede their escape. The tall man produced a small axe from his belt, and with a few expert swings of it, dispatched more of the Brotherhood in the same efficient manner.

Once again on the bridge there was uproar. Soldiers and civilians alike were stumbling blindly to escape the sulphurous fog that the tall man had used to cover his attack and to ease his escape. Beth was now hurled into the back of a two-wheeled cart filled with hay. The tall man leapt up beside her and burrowing in amongst the straw he covered them both, a whip cracked, and the cart sped off, leaving the hurly burly of the bridge in the distance.

The Keeper of the Secrets slumped behind the desk, head in hands, flabbergasted that Fuldus and the girl had slipped through his fingers. He glared at the Oracle with fury burning in his eyes. "Well," he growled, "how did this happen?"

The Oracle looked at him, unmoved by his menacing tone. "As I have said many times," she began, "when dealing with our own kind on this plane, it is impossible to be certain…"

The Keeper interrupted, "Are you going to tell me about raindrops and oceans again?" He barked, "Because my patience is not endless."

The Oracle continued as if he had said nothing, "...we do not occupy a single linear life such as yours, the options are endless," she smiled at him, "unlike your patience," acknowledging that she had heard his previous veiled threat.

"Endless options indeed," he scoffed. "Indulge me then," he said, "can you at least tell me where she is now?"

The Oracle sat upright in her chair and closed her eyes; the room darkened, the air was suddenly filled with sound of horses and distant indistinct chatter. The Keeper looked disturbed, peering around him to see where the ghostly voices were coming from. "What was that?" he blurted, "What does that mean?"

The Oracle was unmoved. Now, the sound of the tiny bell was drifting around the room, but before the Keeper could speak again, the Oracle spoke, "This, as incomplete as it is, is all I hear and see."

The room returned to the way it was previously as the Oracle concluded, "The red man's interference has muddied her mind, I cannot talk with her."

The Keeper of the Secrets could not hide his irritation and reached for the bell on his desk and rang it sharply. The door opened immediately, and a white-robed man entered. "My lord," he stammered nervously.

The man's appearance took the Keeper by surprise. "Where is the Keeper of the Laws?" he barked, but before the man could answer, he was being ushered from the room with, "Find him and send him to me at once," ringing in his ears.

He sat at the desk for five minutes or so before dashing to his feet and racing from the room, yelling at all and sundry to *find the Keeper of the Laws*.

The Oracle now alone surveyed the room and the iron chains that bound the body she occupied. *If only they understood,* she thought, that these things could not contain her. Confinement was not the punishment to her that it was to them. She could feel the wind on her face and the earth beneath her feet whenever she wished, she could close her eyes and travel to snow-capped mountain peaks and sit by thundering waterfalls, she could soar with hawks among rain-filled clouds and stampede with wild horses across seemingly endless grassland.

The sun for her would rise and set a thousand times while they hatched their plans and achieved nothing in a day. The body she occupied while in this room was nothing but a vessel, the most convenient form to converse with them while she was amongst them. She could see it sitting there chained and immobile while she would walk freely.

The cobbles on the bridge were cold to her feet. *The ship, she thought, as unnatural as it was, was quite beautiful.* The resilience of the people of this city made her smile. The market was trading again, children played as dogs barked and the work of the day went on undisturbed. Beyond these city walls, the people behaved in a similar fashion. These small moments of beauty were repeated the world over, not all succumbed to the ways of the Brotherhood and their likes.

Beyond these shores, though, she could see their influence had spread. She could see their new allies massing on the borders of their neighbours. A soldier, mother, child, all to be sacrificed as the indiscriminate machines of war rolled ever onwards. She stood among the uniformed as they plotted from the safety of bunkers, while the lives of others were traded like chess pieces.

She would try and fathom the reasoning and understand the desire that drove them, try and locate the fuel that fed their hatred, look back through their history to see where they lost sight of their commonality. When did they stop seeing their sameness and start to only see their differences? The differences that once were celebrated but were now despised and feared. Lies poured like poison into the ears, until the lies became the truth.

She would sit in rooms at dinner. She would watch them sleep. She had been in churches, temples and sacred spaces. Listened to prayers and incantations, felt love, hope and despair. She had watched birth, marriage and death in every part of this world; it was the same to her eyes. The languages locations and forms of ceremony were different, of course, but the joy and grief were the same, and try as she might, she could still find no reason for the apparent determination of these people to destroy one another and ultimately themselves.

She would find herself back in the body she occupied, and she would weep. *Maybe,* she thought, *this is what this body is after all, it is a vessel, a vessel to contain their grief.*

The Heralds

The cart danced and trundled into the afternoon sun, heading out of the city along side streets and then dirt tracks and country lanes. The journey was a silent one, apart from the clatter of the cartwheels and intermittent sting of the whip. The motion of the cart rocked Beth into a fitful sleep. She would slip out of the day, only to be pulled back in by the scratching on her face of the rough straw which surrounded her.

Onward she went, uphill and down, passing babbling water and the soft mooing of cows. The darkness of night had fallen before the cart finally came to rest. Soft voices began to emerge as the straw was pulled away from her face and she was, this time, gently lifted from the back of the cart. All the haste of her escape now gone, the mood around her was one of calm. Gone were the smells of city, its smoke, the sewage, and its people. The night air was cool and fresh and most welcome.

When Beth opened her eyes fully, she found herself standing outside a picturesque white-washed cottage with heavily scented wisteria growing across the walls and around the door. The cottage itself looked as if it had been grown instead of built, almost obscured by the plants that covered it. Candlelight seeped from its small windows and painted the shingle path pale orange. As the small arched front door opened, a hushed group of six or seven people emerged and ushered her inside. The door was quickly closed behind her.

The room was sparsely furnished, a large oak table and simple chairs stood by an unlit fireplace. The dresser against the wall was empty, no plates nor pots nor pans as one might expect. The walls were plain as were the bare wooden floorboards.

The group moved to the edges of the room encircling Beth, she stood alone, turning slowly to get a first look at their faces, older and more kindly they appeared. There were nine people in the room, as well as the tall man who had taken her from the bridge. It was he who first dropped to his knees and bowed his head, the rest followed immediately after. Beth was confused and a little frightened by the sudden change in mood, then the tall man finally spoke.

"O', fearsome one," he began, "we have waited so long for you." He raised his head slightly and Beth could see tears forming in his watery eyes. He swallowed, his lips quivering as he continued to speak, "We have watched and waited, we had begun to lose hope." The sound of stifled sobs and whimpers from his companions accompanied him. "We of the Order of the Heralds are ready to help you cleanse and deliver this world from those who have defied and defiled you and your sisters."

Beth was now more confused than ever. The blank look on her face stopping the man's speech. There was a moment of silence, all those kneeling around her were looking from one to another, still Beth said nothing. One of the women in the circle shuffled on her knees towards her. Then taking Beth's hands in hers, she looked into her eyes for what seemed an uncomfortably long time. Beth, stared back, hoping for some clue as to who these people were and what they were talking about.

After what seemed like an eternity, the woman finally spoke. She raised her hands and cupped Beth's face. "Oh, child," she said softly, "have you no idea who you are?" Tears were flowing down her face as she turned to the tall man. "It is as we thought," she said, "they have locked her away from herself."

Collective gasps and cries from those assembled animated the room as the tall man stood. "Then we must act quickly to undo this heresy," he hissed, the anger in his voice was becoming more obvious. "Is he here?" he barked.

"Yes," said the woman, "the others were only shortly behind you, their waggon just arrived." With that, the door to the cottage opened and in walked Mrs Cooper from the citadel kitchen, she rushed across the room and threw herself to the floor in front of Beth. Her hands scrabbled around blindly, until they came to rest on Beth's feet.

"Safe at last, my child, safe at last," she said, almost unable to contain her euphoria. She clambered upright and grasped the tall man to her. "Silas," she said, "salvation is at hand, we have him!"

There was a commotion outside, a bustle of shadows filled the doorway as a burly man entered the room with a sack over his shoulder. "We grabbed him in all the confusion," he said, then unceremoniously dumped the sack on the rough floorboards. The contents of the bag groaned, clearly winded and in some discomfort.

Silas looked eagerly at the heap in the middle of the room, "Get him to his feet," he ordered. The sack was instantly made upright and the binding at its top was undone.

The sack began to slip to the floor, a bald head appeared. The dull room was suddenly ablaze with colour, as brilliant and as it was out of place, then standing before them, his nose bloodied and looking shocked and dishevelled, was the Keeper of the Laws.

The tall man, Silas, pulled a chair from the table and sat before the tiny man in red. "Do you know what you have done?" he asked softly. Not waiting for a reply, "you have sinned, affronted the gods you have." He thrust an accusing finger at the man before him as his companions whispered in unison, "Sinner, sinner."

The Keeper of the Laws appeared unmoved, Silas glowered at him. He talked like a kettle on the cusp of boiling. "You can redeem yourself," he said.

"Redeem yourself," the chorus echoed.

Silas took the man's hand, looking, imploring, urging him to agree and somehow see the error of his ways. All he got in return were disdaining looks.

"What is your name, my friend?" asked Silas.

The man in red was taken by surprise, he paused, "I have not had a name for many decades," he replied.

"I understand," said Silas, "you gave yourself over to duty, as have we." Silas gestured to those assembled, "You believed in what you were doing, I do not doubt that." Silas stood, towering over the Keeper of the Laws, "But you, like many, have been lied to." Silas was pacing the room now, keeping his temper in check. "I want you to help us and save yourself, and all those who have been deceived."

The small man in red followed Silas with his eyes as he circled the room. Silas continued, "I know you are not a heretic, that you have been misled, your talents used to further the aims of your master." Silas was now in front of his captive again. "I want you to use those same talents and free the mind of this child." He grasped the Keeper of the Laws by both hands, "You will help us, won't you?"

There was a moment of silence, then a soft chuckle, the two men's eyes met. The Keeper of the Laws was now laughing, almost uncontrollably. "Ha!" he coughed, "Do you mean to kill me with kindness?" Silas' grip on his hands was becoming intense. "First, you call me a sinner, then you want to befriend me whilst appealing to my better nature to save the world," he spluttered. "You think we don't know who you are, Axe-grinder? Or whatever else you may be called this week." The room was sombre, despite the little man's levity, who gulped in air and continued in a more considered tone, "I would not be surprised if the hovel was surrounded already, so prepare to be burned alive, and I, for one, will welcome the flames if it stops me from being tortured by your childlike inanities."

The burly man who had carried the sack into the room darted outside while his companions looked nervously in the direction of the open door. Moments passed, the crunching of feet on gravel could be heard as he strode around the cottage and finally came back in to put all at their ease; they had not been followed and were not surrounded.

Silas rose to his full height, still holding the much smaller man by the hands. In doing so, lifted him a foot or so above the floor. He resembled a fisherman trying to land an impressive but troublesome catch. He looked to the kitchen table and said, "Mrs Cooper, would you open the drawer there and pass me the serrated knife, if you would be so kind?"

Mrs Cooper went to the drawer in a flash, a wince-inducing squeal rent the air as it was opened. "This one, Silas?" she asked, holding a rusted and violent-looking implement before her.

Silas smiled, all the while holding his wriggling catch. "No, my love," he said sweetly, "the bone saw, it's larger, about twelve inches in length, with an oak handle."

Mrs Cooper rattled the unseen contents of the drawer and produced another equally grim-looking object. Silas smiled and nodded. "The very one," he said chirpily. Then stretching his arms to the rafters, he looked at the Keeper of the Laws squarely in the eyes, and in the same unrushed and breezy tone, said, "As I understand it, when you tamper with people's minds and freewill, you hold a small bell between your middle finger and your thumb in one hand," he was walking towards the large kitchen table as he continued to talk. "Likewise, the small hammer is held in the same way by the other hand."

The small man, in one swift motion, was swung upward and brought crashing down onto the table, filling the air with dust. As if reacting to an unspoken command, two other men grabbed him, one by the shoulders and the other the ankles, pinning him in place. Silas reached out a hand and Mrs Cooper furnished him with the bone saw. "So," he giggled excitedly, "as I see it, to go about your work, you have six fingers you don't need."

The Keeper of the Laws shrieked, "You're insane, let me go, I will do whatever you want!" The small man was instantly released.

"You see," said Silas to his companions, "he can be reasonable." He turned back to his prisoner, "And if you still wish to be able to count to ten on your fingers, I suggest you remain that way."

Beth was seated immediately at the centre of the room, as instructed by the Keeper of the Laws. The candles that lit the room were extinguished and everyone present was instructed to remain silent. The tiny bald man, bell and hammer in hand, went about his work. Speaking directly to Beth in hushed secretive tones, he led her through the garden of her dreams and back to the locked rough wooden door. Beth could once more feel the damp earth beneath her feet. Scented air in her nostrils. She was happy and calm. "Place your hand in your pocket, girl," he whispered, "Do you feel the key?" There was a pause. "Yes," came the sleepy response.

"Take the key and place it in the lock," The Keeper of the Laws cast a glance sideways at Silas. He toyed momentarily with telling Beth to destroy the key and stay in the garden forevermore. He was in no doubt though the Axe Grinder would relish removing a few digits, and more if he did. He took a nervous gulp of air, "turn the key," he said with a quiver in his voice.

The door was aglow once more, Beth was ecstatic, the key a searing cold in her hand turned, and the door was gone. "Go," the word jammed in the Keeper's throat, tears soaking his cheeks the enormity of his betrayal of the Brotherhood descending upon him in that instant.

"Forgive me," he sobbed. "You are forgiven," said Beth and she stepped through the door."

She looked down at her feet, aware that the ground on which she was standing was now dissolving, soil and stone becoming a million stars. There was no garden on the other side of the door, just the sky. In the black eternity stars began to dance and swirl around her before silently joining with one another to form one dazzling masse. The light slowly dimmed and began to take shape, a tall luminous figure stepped towards her, shrinking to her height as it did.

The light was completely gone now, and as her eyes adjusted, she could see herself as clearly as if she were looking in a mirror. There she stood looking back at herself, smiling broadly. The two girls embraced until only one remained, and with that Beth found herself standing in the small cottage surrounded by several people she had never before met and a small man she knew only too well. She fixed him with a cold stare. "You are not a nice person," she scolded.

The Keeper looked about him, all the others in the room had thrown themselves to the floor, not daring to look at her. He thought this was probably a wise course of action and joined them.

"Fearsome one," came a voice at her feet, "may I look upon you?"

Beth glanced about her, a tall man lying face down was the one speaking. "Fearsome one," she laughed. "Please get off the floor," she urged them all. They clambered from their bellies to their knees, and there they stayed.

"My name is Silas," but before he could continue his introduction, Beth cut him off.

"You are the one they call Silas," she said, "Ned the Knife, the Axe Grinder." Beth's smile had drained away, "You are the leader of a group known as the Heralds." The others in the room gasped and murmured to one another, astonished that the girl knew so much.

"I am he, fearsome one," said the man. "I and my brothers and sisters have waited so long; we have watched for you for so long!" The man was becoming hysterical, and those with him were nodding in fervent agreement. "We are ready to aid you in punishing the wicked and cleanse this earth with fire and fury!"

He fell silent, eyes wide, like an overeager child with spittle on his chin. Beth was in equal measures, tickled and horrified by his outburst. "I am afraid," she began, "you have waited in vain."

Confused, he looked to his companions, and they to him. "You are the scourge of this earth, the one promised, the Desolator, are you not?" he sheepishly enquired.

Beth seated herself. "I will be whatever I need to be," she said sternly. There was an uneasy but short silence before she spoke again. "Yourselves and the Brotherhood are not so different, Axe Grinder," she mused. There was a collective intake of breath. "You both have a plan for this world," she said, "but neither of you thought to ask if anybody, other than you and your followers want to be part of it." She laughed. "The Brotherhood want everyone who do not do as they want them to: dead, and you," tapping Silas playfully on the nose, "want everyone to burn for not doing as you think I want them to."

The room remained in a stunned silence. Beth looked at those kneeling before her, "Please get off the floor," she implored. Everyone duly obliged. "Silas," she said, "you and your friends have been very helpful, if it were not for you, I would still be locked inside this body." She turned to the Keeper of the Laws. "You asked for forgiveness, but not from me." The man in red took a step away from her. "I do not believe your Brothers in white will see your act of self-preservation as a thing to be applauded." The Keeper could see the truth of her words.

Before he could offer an opinion though, Beth continued to speak, "As I said before, I do forgive you," the small man visibly relaxed, "but," she said, "you will tamper with no one else's mind."

"I absolutely will not," promised the small man in red bowing gracefully. Beth smiled, "I don't believe you." Then with the faintest of touches, the brush of one finger to his forehead, he collapsed in a slumbering heap. "You will stay like that until this…" she paused, and pursed her lips looking for the right words, "…this matter is resolved." She turned to Silas, "I would suggest you put the little man in his bag and put him back where you found him before the Brotherhood comes looking."

The Keeper of the Laws was swiftly packed up and placed gently back on the cart, and with no ceremony at all he was on his way back to Fulham. Beth was sitting on the kitchen table, swinging her legs back and forth humming to herself as Silas and the Heralds reassembled. "Silas," she began, "it would seem you and your followers have been on something of a fool's errand. You need to find a way to better serve this world." With that she jumped down on to the floor, "Change is coming," she said and bid them farewell. She walked past them without uttering another word. They watched her brush past the wisteria at the doorway, some of the petals fell about her as she went and seemed to follow where she walked. They swirled and danced in a spiral, surrounding her, until she could no longer be seen. Then like a mist on a summer morning, the suns warmth dissolved her, and she was gone.

The Desolator

The market in Fulham was setting up shop as usual. Nothing, it appeared, including the destruction of the bridge on which it had stood for years, or even the return of the Brotherhood, stood in the way of the sale of fresh fruits and vegetables. Those whose businesses had been destroyed had begun to rebuild and carried on trading in ramshackle lean-tos and tents.

It was now viewed as a miracle. No one, it appeared, had died on the bridge during its bombardment, with the exception of the dozen or so of the Brotherhood's soldiers dispatched by an unknown assailant. The previous evening, the ale and pie house, 'The Drunken Porter', was awash with hair-raising tales of escape from tumbling masonry and whistling artillery.

As for the identity of the knife-throwing assassin, as much as everyone *knew* who was most likely the culprit, none dared say it aloud, and with good reason, for that morning as the market reconvened, Silas, Ned the Knife, the Axe Grinder was back plying his trade as if nothing out of the ordinary had occurred the day prior.

The citadel was now flying the white flags of the Brotherhood and the double-headed dragon of the Scandinavians. Many of the general staff continued about their duties as they would on any workday. Breakfast was prepared and cleaned away with military precision and lunch was already well in hand. The Keeper of the Secrets had not left the office Fuldus used to occupy since his arrival.

"Well," he spat towards the still-chained Oracle, "have you any news on the whereabouts of the Keeper of the Laws yet?"

The Oracle could not help but snort. "Yes," she smiled, "he is in the market." She could see the large cloth sack tied at the top and resting unnoticed by a waggon loaded with potatoes and other vegetables. Still sleeping, he was retrieved and brought before his now irate leader.

"What's wrong with him?" he impatiently snapped at the still amused Oracle.

"He is merely sleeping, so he can do no more harm with his bells and incantations," he was told, "and no, I can't wake him before you ask."

The Keeper of the Secrets continued to pepper her with questions, but to his almost all-consuming rancour, the Oracle had fallen into silence too. She could see him screaming at her, it was as if she was looking through a frosted glass window, the kind popular in the many alehouses of the city. It was as if she were inside, and he were standing in the street. She just could not hear him any longer, something for which she found herself immeasurably grateful.

The Oracle looked about, she was now in another room completely. It was impossibly white and seemingly never ending. There were two large wingback chairs of white leather, and a small circular white marble table. The ceiling was high and intricately carved with flowers and cherubs, and the floor was highly polished white-washed planks, as for the walls they were barely visible off in some infinite distance.

Of the two chairs, the one facing her was empty, but from the other came a soft voice, "Won't you come and join me? It's been so long since I have spoken with us."

The Oracle found herself seated in the vacant chair, and there, smiling from the other side of the table, was Beth.

The Oracle instantly transformed and became a child of roughly the same age as her companion. Tears fell freely from her eyes, but her joy was obvious. The two children clasped one another's hands and did not speak for several minutes, perhaps hours, or even days.

The Oracle-child finally broke the silence. "I felt you as soon as you were released, I knew they would not be able to hold you indefinitely. Where are you now? Beth looked confused. "I am here with you," she said, but now unsure of her answer.

It was the Oracle's turn to smile this time. "Our spirit is free to wander from the physical whenever it chooses." She gave Beth's upper arm a gentle pinch, from which she pulled away, looking slightly cross. "This body is not real," laughed the Oracle, "it's an illusion." With that, she became an old man, then almost immediately, a boy and then back to the girl she was before. "When we are here, we can be whatever suits us. The pain you think you just felt is part of the human condition."

The Oracle knew to continue, "When we are in human form, we are afflicted with some of their traits. Our physical self can be restrained or have pain inflicted upon it. When we are human, we are subject to their fears also. The fear of pain being inflicted upon us, or those about whom we care, and consequently, the fear of death is also very real."

The Oracle child was crying again, this time with a different cause. "My other self," she sobbed, "was in such agony and I could do nothing." Beth gave her a comforting embrace, even though she now realised she was doing no such thing. "That is how," the Oracle continued, "we have been so maliciously used to further their ends."

After a pause to compose herself, she said with a smile, "That's enough of my snivelling and self-pity, I think we need to discuss why you were sent there." The Oracle was once again the old woman who had first joined Beth at the table. "You, my love," she whispered, "have the hardest decision of us all to make."

Beth knew this to be true. "Has this choice been made before?" she asked.

"Many times," came the reply. "From slight alterations to beginning again." The old woman was staring deep into Beth's eyes and gently holding both her hands. "It is an awful weight to carry, we realise that there is so much good in them, but you have seen and experienced first-hand the lengths to which they will go in order achieve their ends."

Beth remained silent understanding exactly what her companion meant. "You, my love, could spend an eternity debating with them and still be as far from reconciling their need to exist and their apparent insatiable thirst for war and destruction, but that is what you must do, reconcile the irreconcilable."

"Why was a child sent to do this?" asked Beth. "We thought," said the Oracle, "that if you grew amongst them, you would gain better insight than our occasional interactions have given in the past, but they, instead of nurturing you, choose to corrupt."

The Oracle appeared impossibly old now, the discussion seemed to be almost too hard to continue with. "We have found ourselves at crossroads such as these before. Now, in the future and the past. In some ways the decision has already be made, but whenever the decision is made, it still must be made by someone, for the first time, and that, my poor girl, on this occasion, is you."

Beth understood only one thing for certain, there were no easy answers. If she had indeed already made her decision, why did she not know what it was? *How was she,* she thought, *to resolve a riddle that had not yet been posed to her?*

The Oracle could see the inner workings of Beth's mind. "Do not mire yourself in thought," she counselled. "Answers will come, but for now we must leave," said the Oracle, "We are no longer where we were, and I fear time and events have marched on while you and I have been talking." All Beth now had was the old woman's voice. "But before we go, I will tell you the one certainty I have come to realise over the ages."

Her voice was strong and unfaltering, "They fear one thing," she said, "more than any other, more so even than us. More than war, famine, or even death, and that is change. When the need to change and grow becomes apparent, those in power will rather fall back into toxic nostalgia to justify oppression and intolerance; they proffer the return to a past which never existed. Intransigence, you see, is the real tragedy of human existence, they would rather die than change, and therein lies their dilemma, for without change, they will surely die."

The Oracle finished with her thoughts and looked about her. She was no longer in the office in Fulham. The last day she remembered was fair and calm. Today was stormy and onerous. She found herself now in a tent full of men, canvas being pounded by the rain. It was one tent amongst many. Countless tents packed in neat rows across the lush fields of the Gaulish coast. Time it seemed, had indeed marched on.

In the distance, the thunder of the sea churned by gales hammered the shoreline. Dark clouds scudded across the sky, at such a speed that one would think they were migrating birds in search of better weather. The sun had not shown itself all day and now night was falling.

Campfires danced frantically in the wind raging against the oncoming darkness, as the uniformed army of the Brotherhood crowded in for some warmth and comfort. Steaming pots of tea bubbled and hissed, while smoke carried the smell of bacon and sausage.

The camp was positioned on the hills surrounding a city of several thousands. It was the first of many towns and cities in Gaul to fall to the Brotherhood and their growing numbers. Stories of the horrors visited on those who tried to defend their families, homes and beliefs spread quickly throughout the regions and the rest of the country, making their advance much quicker than they had anticipated.

The lands with which Gaul shared borders met the same fate. The first cities all but destroyed as a warning to the others not to resist. The Spaniards to the south and the Germanic to the north found themselves with new rulers in a matter of months. The success of the campaign thus far had emboldened the Keeper of the Secrets to leave Fulham in his now familiar white paddle steamer and join with his commanders in the field. He eagerly read reports from smaller garrisons who had been sent further south and east into the desert lands. They had reported back declaring them a hive of savages and heathen worshippers of false gods. The troop's numbers were reinforced massively and sent with the moral imperative to save the foreigners from themselves. The people who lived there in ornate sandstone cities, if not accepting of the Brotherhood, were slaughtered, their temples burned, and their lands plundered.

The Keeper of the Secrets stood hunched over a map of the known world, as the wind continued to howl and tear at the tent around him, it was as if it were alive, twitching and writhing like a tethered beast trying to break free from its shackles. The only object in the room unaffected by the wind was the iron cage to which the unfortunate Oracle found herself once more confined.

The Keeper ran his bony finger along lines delineating borders between countries. Over mountains, oceans, cities and farmlands. "Nowhere," he declared to those assembled, "does the white flag of the Brotherhood not fly!" He raised his head as a ripple of applause ran around the group of thirty or so generals and admirals. "Please," he said humbly, "I should be congratulating all of you, these great achievements are yours also." There was murmuring and muttering, and cheery voices raised in agreement, and then more applause.

"We stand here tonight," he continued, "masters of all we survey, no army dares oppose us, our victory all but complete." The crowd was now cheering and stamping, a raised hand silenced them once more. The old man stepped back and seated himself in the large cushioned chair, which was directly behind him. "How is it then," he said, "with dominion over this earth, you can still not bring before me the one thing which still vexes me, the child known as Little Death?"

The merriment of the room evaporated, flapping canvas the only sound. "One child," the Keeper growled, "one child can evade an entire army." Anxious generals glanced at one another, none daring to speak aloud. "Not a whiff of her, it's nearly a year since she was spirited out of the city." His ire was evident in every word, "and be in no doubt that it was her who sent the Law Keeper back to me a gibbering wreck, and you all stand there in silence."

"My lord," came a voice from the back of the tent, barely audible over the roar of the wind. "My lord," it came again, those in front of the man speaking began to separate as he walked towards the Keeper of the Secrets. The Keeper's eyes narrowed to get a better view of the one approaching. "My lord," he said again, "if I may offer the opinion of the scholars' present."

The Keeper was intrigued enough not to shout the man into silence. "You may," he said. The room was hushed now, except for the incessant howling of the wind.

"You have said, my lord," he began, "the child has not been seen since her interference with the Keeper of the Laws." He turned and gestured to a small group of bookish, bespectacled men at the back of the tent. "It is our opinion that the child, now free of her earthly shackles," pausing to catch a nervous breath before continuing, he said as emphatically as possible, "she has left this realm and returned to her own."

The Keeper pulled himself upright in his seat. "And what, may I ask, brings you to that conclusion?" he said, casting his gaze to those cowering at the back of the tent.

Their spokesman quickly spluttered, "Well, my lord, her inaction."

The seated man paused and drummed his fingers on the maps in front of him for a few moments, then slowly, the words began to form. He closed his eyes, his lips curling as he did. "You," he began, "you and your learned friends surmise that because she has not been seen nor made an attempt to intervene in our affairs," he shook his head incredulously, his mouth moving but no words, just huffs and gasps. The scholars were shuffling nervously, like chickens who could hear a fox at their henhouse door. "She has just lost interest in us, and," shouted the Keeper, who was on his feet now, bellowing to make himself heard above the wind, "she has just gone home!"

The scholar bravely stood his ground. "My lord, all the evidence, all scripture shows that if the Desolator were indeed amongst us, we would already have been," pausing to find the best word, he blurted out, "punished."

"Punished," sneered the Keeper, "By punished, I assume you mean begging for our lives before being flayed, slaughtered and incinerated?"

The man nodded. "Yes, my lord!" he yelled. The Keeper and all else were taken aback by the forcefulness of his response. "My lord," he continued, "I apologise, I did not mean to raise my voice so," he gave a small bow as to appease his master. The Keeper raised his hand and glanced around him. The canvas of the tent was no longer being torn at and pulled in all directions by the wind, there was silence.

"If I may offer an alternative opinion," came a soft voice from behind him.

The Keeper turned slowly and glared. "Awake from your stupor, at last," he hissed at the Oracle. Her silence over the past months had nearly sent her to the Maiden, so incensed by it had he become. "And after all this time, with what insight do you wish to gift us?"

The old woman smiled. "Just this," she said, "the child is here."

The room was suddenly alive, men looked nervously over their shoulders. One even crouched and looked under the table in front of the Keeper. A scholar, a short rotund man of a particularly nervous disposition, stifled a small shriek before fainting.

The Oracle could not supress her smile. "The child is here," she repeated more forcefully, before adding with relish, "as is the Desolator you fear so much."

The Oracle placed her hands on the bars of the cage. They began to glow, lighting the tent like a thousand lanterns. The cage was consumed by it and then it was gone. The occupant was still engulfed by the same light and being transformed by it. Those assembled shielded their eyes, transfixed, the light was blinding, fierce, white and cold. The tent slowly began to darken around the Keeper and his company who stood blinking and incredulous, frozen in fear as there now standing in the old woman's place, was the child Little Death.

"Please," she said softly, "don't be alarmed." As she stepped forwards, all before her made a slight retreat.

The Keeper finally found his voice. "Guards!" he howled. None were forthcoming.

Little Death stepped before the Keeper. "As usual," she said, "you have been unable to see what was under your nose all along." She gazed about the tent at the generals, admirals and scholars, some cowering whilst others bristled with rage. Every argument they had ever had, every belief they had ever held, all their bias and intolerance, etched in each of the crags and lines of their faces. Their beliefs worn like armour, impervious to argument or reason. "What a sad collection of old men," she sighed, "it's no wonder your world is ready to devour itself."

General huffing and puffing greeted her every word, but she, having no need of their approval, carried on regardless. "You should be at home playing with your grandchildren, not out here planning ways to make a new generation of orphans and widows."

The Keeper of the Secrets finally found his voice and seething with a compound of rage and fear, he began to spit words back at her, "We have no intention of devouring our world, that's why you're here, that's why I have dedicated my life to foiling your plans!"

Little Death cared no more for his rage than she did his rationale. She looked to him, asking, "Do you know why we sent a child to play this part?" She studied the blank expressions, papery skin, watery eyes and bloated egos. "Well?" she asked again. The crowd remained silent, "We hoped you would find some sympathy in your sour hearts for a child and consequently, for yourselves and others." She meandered through the tent, yet every time she neared one of them, they would shy away, as if she were a branding iron being held too close for comfort.

Little Death walked from the tent, she stood just outside, and asked those still inside to join her. Slowly, they obliged. The sudden appearance of a furiously animated Keeper was causing a large crowd to gather around them. Thousands of bodies began to crush in to see what was going on. "Look at these people," said the girl, "you could have found a thousand better ways to employ them. Doctors, builders, poets, artist." She shook her head at the short-sightedness of it all.

The Keeper was now only to aware of the multitude of faces staring at him. "Get these men back to their billets," he ordered. His bodyguard forming a wall between him and the conscripts, began to push them back. The crowd shuffled down the hill, order was begrudgingly returning to the camp. The men, though, kept their distance, and continued to watch and listen. "You see, sheep," he scoffed. "If it was not for me, they would wander this hillside grazing and falling foul of the wolves and bears."

He was speaking now with the conviction of a man who believed every word he was saying. "I give them purpose, I raise them out of their pointless lives. I offer them a chance to be a part of something greater than themselves. If not for me, they would still be wallowing in mud and killing each other over rustled cattle!" He turned to Little Death, "Without purpose these people would simply rot like unharvested potatoes."

"Do you really hold your brothers and sister in such low regard?" she asked. "Did you have parents, or like us, were you found under a tree during a storm?"

The Keeper sneered, "I am nothing like you, and they are nothing like me."

The girl shook her head in despair. "It helps you to think of other people as lesser than you. How else would you make the decisions you do? How would you sleep at night if you cared for anyone of them?"

The old man rolled his eyes in disdain of her sentiment. "I have built a world where they have a place and a purpose," he said.

"You have built a world controlled by an angry child spinning a top," she interrupted, "It won't topple so long as you continue to land the lashes it needs to keep it turning."

The Keeper pointed to the rows and rows of tents. "If you care so much for these people, why are you here to destroy them?" he barked.

Little Death looked at him, her eyes narrowed. "I can't be certain if you really don't understand, or just chose not to," she said softly. Her calm demeanour riled him even further.

"I understand perfectly well!" he screamed. Little Death knew she was wasting her breath, she had heard enough and brushed past him and his guards. She vanished into the sea of soldiers who swarmed to catch a glimpse the child who had so rattled the mighty Keeper of the Secrets.

She looked at them, their sunken faces and haunted eyes made her heart ache. "You have had your lives stolen from you," she said quietly. Her words surged around the camp, as if she were speaking to each of them individually. "You need to see your world, you need to feel the pain you inflict on one another, you need to know how others feel, you need to see where the path you have been set upon leads." The throng of bodies was beginning to thin out, and she found herself standing alone. She gazed upon the thousands of faces and whispered, "I am sorry," and with that, *she fell to her knees and forced her hands into the earth.*

The ground beneath their feet trembled as the sky above their heads split asunder, it was as if a giant box was being torn open and coloured water was being poured down its sides from above. The world around them dissolved, becoming an ethereal cloud before flattening into streaked and smudged layers of shimmering glassy reality. On to each, images began to form. Panic was spreading amongst those watching, but none could move, hemmed in as they were by the new world forming around them.

Little Death was no longer alone on her knees, she was now one of four figures with their hands buried in the earth: an old woman, a young boy and an old man had magically joined her.

The soldiers standing in front of Little Death looked on petrified. Before the young boy was a tented camp, ablaze, terrified screams lacerating the air, the banners of *their* army flying over the carnage. The old woman knelt before snow-capped mountains and glistening forests, but her people forced to live in squalor, starving, while self-destructive despair stole away their will to live. The old man on a sterile city street, alone and anguished, while a beautifully manicured but uncaring world rushed by.

The Keeper of the Secrets and his generals cowered on the hillside behind their troops, as the kaleidoscope of images took shape and solidified. Time and distance dissolved it was as if all the days of world were colliding and happening at once.

Cities were stacked on top of jungles, exotic beasts long extinct, strode across snowy plains with gorillas and lions. Icy waterfalls, rain forests, tropical rivers and traffic-choked roads intertwined. The past, present and the future laying one over the other. Canoes were paddled as rockets blasted to the stars. Steam trains rattled across prairies now occupied by wandering tribes of hunter-gatherers.

There were gleaming towers in glass city landscapes where offices workers looked now on ziggurats atop dizzying mountains. A cluster of adobe huts in a sun-scorched desert filling the sky above them. The occupants able to walk from one place to another, from one time to another. They would smile and greet each other before the world would change around them once more and pull them apart.

The wealthy, the starving, young, old, the dead and those yet to be born, a million, million faces staring at each other in disbelief and awe. The images kept changing, lush pasture would unfurl like a shimmering carpet as forests blazed, and mountains would crumble, cities taking their place, only to be washed away by raging oceans.

Then over shimmering horizons, armies marched crashing into one another. Infantrymen facing down armoured tank divisions. Stone axes clashing with bayonets and swords, a blizzard of arrows as an answer to Gatling gun fire. Sleek warplanes screamed past the terrified pilots of hot air balloons. The sky became a patchwork of vapour trails as rockets rained down delivering white-hot blinding explosions and thunderous searing tornados scorched the earth sparing nothing, buildings, animals, or people.

The Brotherhoods troops joined a terrified stampede as those fleeing the searing heat clawed and clambered over one another to make their escape, but there was nothing only the blinding light and a throng of anguished hopeless faces. Silence fell like a shroud over the memory of lives, the history of the past and future and the spectre of the earth as it faded.

The screams of millions being carried on the wind through the ages to drift into nothing. All that remained was blackened soot, the land smoked and smouldered. The few survivors scrabbled over the wasteland, blind and diseased, a raw poisonous wind picking at their bones, and the carcass of the planet they had destroyed.

The sun finally set, and the sky went dark. Their earth was no more and all that was left to mourn its passing were the distant cold stars.

The darkness began to lift, and a more familiar landscape took shape. The sun peered through the clouds shining down on the hillside where the army of the Brotherhood stood just as before, with its neat rows of tents, and its white flags dancing in the breeze.

The four kneeling figures raised their heads and spoke in unison. "From the moment you arrive screaming into existence, to the end of your days, you are taught to fear one another. That you are as different from one another as you are from the birds in the sky and the fish in the ocean." The Keeper was stumbling down the hillside with his entourage in hot pursuit. He forced his way through the crowds and was now standing facing Little Death. She paid no heed and continued, "You are kept isolated from each other, made to fight for what you are told is rightfully yours at the expense of others, but this earth is not just meant for the shrewd and powerful."

The Keeper was screaming at Little Death and urging the ranks of men not to listen, his guards pushing them, striking at them, ordering them back to their tents. They were not to be moved. Her voice continued to speak to everyone directly, "You have a choice, you can follow these men, or you can find a new way, you *can* change. Your lives here are so short, yet they could be so rich in joy and love, more than you would need to fill all eternity."

There was momentary silence, just enough for the Keeper to make himself heard. "You think I will allow you to destroy all I have achieved? That the whim of a girl will decide their future?" he roared. Turning back to the men, he screamed, "She is here to deceive you and destroy us all!"

Not a soul moved, Little Death smiled, alone once more. "The whim of a girl," she repeated. "Would my words be more worthy if I were a man?" she asked, her voice rumbling as she did. She reached out her tiny hands towards the Keeper, grasping him by the shoulders, her fingers biting into him, and lifting him from the ground. He was dangling in the air, her fingers becoming a vices grip, her frame massive; she was gone and there, standing before him, was Fuldus.

"We had our chance," he said, "to make this world in our own image, now what does it look like?" He craned his head, left and right surveying the forlorn, displaced fathers and mothers, the farmers, teachers and shopkeepers. "It's an ugly, hateful place we have created," his voice mirroring the grim reality surrounding them. "You talked of purpose and achievement, but what did we achieve? We played at life, we connived life, we fought life, but we never lived it. We failed old man, we could no more bend this earth to our will than we could teach fleas to whistle," he laughed. "We were so consumed by our own arrogance that we could see nothing else." He placed the Keeper gently back to his feet and took a deep breath of salty air. "We strutted around trying to make order and meaning, you and I, we should have realised we were not only wasting our time, but ourselves as well."

With that he was gone as quickly as he had appeared. Beth stood before the Keeper again. "Hatred," she said, "is an unnatural state of being, it cannot, and will not be allowed to continue." She took him by the hands. He dropped to his knees before her, like the exhausted old man he was. She smiled sweetly, "You have no place here, this world needs to move on without you and your kind. You represent the past, a past that has subverted the joys of life to a twisted caricature."

The Keeper remained silent, Beth leaned in and whispered, "You fear me as the Desolator?" The old man still said nothing. "I am not the one this world should fear." Wanting him to understand there was no malice in her words, she paused as one might, before delivering bad news to an ageing relative, and said, "I was sent here to stop the Desolator." Then after glancing around her at the generals, admirals and back to the Keeper, she whispered, "I was sent here to stop you."

The Keeper appeared so frail now that Little Death helped him to his feet. She gestured to the Keeper of the Secrets and his generals and admirals, "Do not hate these men," she said to those listening. "I know their crimes are enormous and too many to ever imagine forgiving, but that is what you must learn to do." The multitude of soldiers bayed for blood regardless, shaking their fists and hurling abuse. Sods of earth began to rain down around them. She raised her hand. "Please," she said disdainfully, "are you so innocent?"

Her voice in their ears was more insistent than before, the soothing tone was gone. "You are not children," she said, "You did not have to do as you were told." The grumbles of dissent began to quiet. "You have blood on your hands too," she reminded them. A culpable silence began to spread through the ranks. She gazed at the crowds with tears in her eyes. "You are being given the most amazing gift," she said, "a second chance."

Little Death looked to the Keeper. "I hope someone will shed a tear for you when you are gone, it must be a terrible thing to be unloved." Her voice was in his head alone now, "To face the end without a kind word from those around you, no smiles in the remembering of you, surely that must show you how your life has been wasted."

Little Death addressed the crowd once more, "The men and women who helped create this world, The Brotherhood and their Sisters, I know it will seem unfair, but they are to receive an even greater gift than you can possibly imagine."

She gripped the Keeper and the nearest officer she could reach by the hands, "You are coming with me," she said with a mischievous smile. Some of the generals began to dart through the crowd attempting to escape, Little Death shook her head and laughed softly.

The sky was clear now, and the sun warmed the crowds beneath it. Little Death summoned a gentle breeze, and as it brushed past those watching, sending petals and leaves disappearing over the horizon, the generals, the admirals, the Keeper of the Secrets and Little Death vanished with them.

Epilogue

The soldiers who had found themselves in foreign lands mostly returned home. Some did not, enamoured with warmer weather, new faces and ways of life. Some never left, finding new homes and families. Those who did return found life on the islands, like elsewhere had moved on. In time villages became towns and towns became cities. The cities formed states and states formed nations.

Those who witnessed the events of that day became less in number. As it is with all great wars, those who took part succumb to age with the passage of time, and their voices are lost. Their stories become hearsay. Fuldus and his kin were forgotten, as were the Brotherhood and their collective deeds. The Children of Summer were rarely, if ever, mentioned.

In schools, they teach that there came a day, a day the world, when faced with a choice, to perish or change, choose the latter. Why? Why did they make that choice? Because of a girl called Little Death. But she like many details became lost. She became a fanciful notion, a metaphor for common sense and the realisation that life does not have to be defined by greed, political manoeuvring and conflict.

Yet, even now, people will still tell wild tales of walking in meadows and forests in the heat of a summer evening, where they have met the strangest of strangers. Twin sisters who have told their fortunes with such a degree of accuracy, it took their breath away. Others have told of women who have opened windows in the world and let them walk in jasmine-scented gardens with the most beautiful children you have ever seen, and they were still home in time for bed.

While others talk of a girl, a girl who dances in a whirlwind of blossom and petals. She appears like a shadow and dissolves like a mist warmed by the first rays of sun on a summer morning. She is radiant, immaculate, and always dressed in white. She has slightly tanned skin and smooth dark hair. Her features are small, her lips red. The tips of her ears projecting slightly through her hair in a most appealing fashion, but it's her eyes that captivate you. Eyes of the darkest wet brown, like molasses. It's almost impossible to tell the pupil and iris apart. But that, they say, is not even the most striking thing about her. It is said, should you be lucky enough to be taken by the hands to dance with her in a whirlwind of blossom, don't be surprised when you see that she has dirt under her fingernails.

The End

Lightning Source UK Ltd.
Milton Keynes UK
UKHW021406140420
361682UK00015B/3812

9 781528 925792